Spirit War

Theodora Maeve Conole

Copyright © 2023 Theodora Conole
All rights reserved.
ISBN: 9798870746999

·for my family, who is always there·

Chapter 1. The Park

I sat, zombie-like, on the green park bench. It was ugly. It was uncomfortable. It was home. I was thinking, maybe I'd been there hundreds of times?

No, I revised, probably a thousand.

It was unusually cool for a day in August, but it was buggy. My younger siblings played and laughed angelically on the park structure, which was made of faded wood. Despite my grouchy attitude this morning, I couldn't resist thinking how cool the park was. It was totally handcrafted.

Every other park I'd been to had nowhere near the unique feeling ours had, for they were all stocky and modern. This park, my park, almost felt like it was a part of the thick woods surrounding it.

The balance beams became logs, the columns were trees and the swinging bridges became glowing leafy canopies. Though the park was old, it was still a thriving forest. And today my two younger siblings were the animals.

"Blair, c'mon, play with us," Magnolia whined. The few minutes they were lost in the game were precious to me, but now I had to deal with their pleas. "You promised you'd play, remember?" Her dark hair is medium length, and her caramel eyes shimmer with love, so irresistible. And she's right, I did promise. It was more like a bribe to keep her quiet when we were leaving the house — so she wouldn't wake up my one-year-old brother.

"Yeah, you promised!" Luna, who was two years younger than Monnie, said huffily, going along with whatever Monnie said. They looked ghastly similar, except for Luna's longer hair and her eyes were more dark-chocolate.

"But I'm so-" I found my mouth widening with a yawn. "Tired."

"You're always so tired these days," pouted Monnie.

"Mm-hmm," agreed Luna instantly. "Please, Bee-Bee?" My youngest sister contorted her face in perhaps the cutest way humanly possible, as if using my nickname wasn't enough already. The way her chocolate eyes kept doubling and her lip jutted out . . .

"Oh, fine," I sighed offhandedly. It was no use to resist the littles.

Quickly, I was whirled into their complex game, but it was also simple and silly. Filled with pretty princesses, brave knights and, my favorite, grumpy dragons.

It took forever for the game to meet its end but eventually, it slowed down. Each second that ticked by filtered another heat blast into the air, and soon it was sickeningly hot, humidity swarming around us like it was trying to mimic the mosquitos. Monnie's face was tomato red and Luna's glistening black hair was plastered to her neck with sweat. I was dying to go back to an air-conditioned house, but I knew Monnie and Luna didn't want to stop playing.

Finally I surrendered to the heat. "Okay, guys. Let's start heading home, alright?" I panted. Was it actually possible to die from heat stroke?

"Aww, it's not that bad," they frowned, sad to leave the park and the game, but I was already walking away. How had the heat come so swiftly? I thought. So much for a cool day, I thought again, and scowled.

And just like that, my grumpiness returned. Eased for a while by little kid pretend-play, it was now crawling back annoyingly, making every tiny thing seem huge and bad. Monnie and Luna were walking too slow. It was too hot. My mosquito bites itched. And why, why, WHY was my house so far away?

Normally, the walk from my house to the park felt like nothing but a little step. Reality, it was probably around 0.1 miles. But now the smothering heat and slow five- and three-year-old who trailed behind me were making it seem to take hundreds of years.

"Please hurry up," I called gruffly behind me. Ever since I'd turned thirteen, I'd somehow become the permanent babysitter, which I normally loved, but sometimes it bugged me at times like these. I twisted my midnight hair deathly tight until we finally arrived home.

My house was tall and spiral-like. With the washed-out limestone bricks and towering structure, it always reminded me slightly of the castles Magnolia and Luna were fascinated by. The landscaping though, was another story. The browned grass laid defeated and matted on the soggy mud. The sidewalk was a sad beige and it was cracked. And the bushes were mangy and uneven, desperate for a cut.

But for some reason, both my parents didn't care at all. Maybe they thought it was just too hopeless, a lost cause, but that didn't sound like them at all. They were the crafty, handy sort of people who were truly convinced, 'You can do anything if you put your mind to it'.

My parents, Sebastian and Celeste Cameron were both weirdly fit for parents; my mom was a health nut and my dad was an exercise fanatic. They had a lot in common. Black hair and sunny brown eyes. Tanned skin and the same craftspeople spirit. Grossly enough, sometimes they were even confused as siblings or cousins. No thank you!

They also held the same religious beliefs. Their moms and dads, (A.K.A, my grandparents), belonged to the same House, called Wind Nation which honors the majestical sky gods and belongs to the wind element. The legend says, thousands of years ago, there was some magical power source given as a gift from the sky gods that gave each of the Wind Nation people wowing spirit animals to use if needed.

These tales always sounded to me as if it was a part from Monnie and Lunas' pretend play, but my mom and dad were so passionate it was hard to doubt them.

"The sky gods were so very generous to us, to give us the power source. But the gods foresaw evil troops coming to steal it for themselves!" my dad explained. At this point, my parents' eyes filled with life and their mouths floated into slight smiles, probably recalling the way their parents had told them the same stories.

"So, one day," my mom continued, "the loneliest god of all, but the most powerful, the god of night; named Luna—"

"That's me!" Luna would squeal, her grin too big for her face.

"Yes, you were named after the goddess of night, Luna." My mom smiled warmly, sweeping her salt and pepper hair over her shoulder. "Anyway, the gods saw that we didn't stand a chance against the evil troops. So they sent Luna, the sneakiest of them all, down to earth to teach the Wind Nation how to harness the full power of the power source, which was how to become the spirit animals.

"But little did they know, Luna was still mad with the sun god about something that had happened between them. But he was still the ruler, and no one could disobey him. So she did what she was told and taught the people how to harness the full power of the source and they all became able to transform into their spirit animals . . . but then she did something unthinkable. She handed the power source over to their allies, the sea gods saying that it was a gift. And they took it to the bottom of the ocean."

"Yes," Dada said, nodding forlornly. "The gods were furious with her when she returned. At least the evil troops turned away, uninterested. But the gods were so mad they became determined to steal it back!"

"And eventually they did. But sadly, with a decade underwater, the power source had lost almost all connection to the spirit world. Only the strongest spirit survived: the dragon spirit."

The story was interesting and my personal favorite. I could picture the shadowy but beautiful Luna sneaking across the stars, the fuming other gods waiting for her with rage-filled purple faces. And, most of all, I could see the powerful, glimmering dragons flapping their majestic wings and their scales shimmering colorfully like diamonds in the light.

I walked into the house, sweating as visions and legends swam in my head. My mom and dad sat bed-headed and sleepy-eyed at the sturdy kitchen table my mom built herself. It was in great condition still except for a few chips my oldest sibling Eleanor gave it as a child having a tantrum.

She had a hard head.

And Atticus, don't forget to add him to the picture. As a feisty one year-old, his face was a perfect twirl of mischievousness and innocence. His random tufts of light brown hairs stood straight up. As his chubby legs stuck out of his highchair, my parents tried to coax food into his tiny mouth, but he whacked it back into their faces.

I smiled, too tired to laugh, but everyone else did. The sound was light and sweet and joyful, and I cherished the moment. But the tiredness was weighing me down so greatly. A burden, dragging me the opposite way I wanted to go.

"You know what?" I announced, surrendering to my body. "I think I'm going to take a quick nap."

If we were in a movie, that soundtrack would've screeched to a stop, silent with suspense and screaming with awkwardness. Maybe it was a touch weird to take a nap at ten o'clock in the morning, but I was a growing girl! None of their business.

"Why?" My dad asked bluntly. He probably thought I was joking.

"Subtle, Dad," I rolled my eyes playfully. It took a lot.

"Are you feeling alright, Blair? Did something happen, are you feeling sick?" My mom instantly went into Protective Mama Mode. Her eyes flickered with fear, her face creased into a bunch of little lines.

"Mom, I'm fine," I said tightly. "Just a little tired." Little was an understatement. I wanted to pass out and sleep for one-thousand years. This wasn't helping.

"Ya! She said she was too tired to play with us!" Monnie cut in snippily, scowling.

"Mm-hmm," echoed her little twin.

"But I did, remember?" I reminded them desperately. "And I had fun, too."

Raising a bushy eyebrow, my dad frowned. "But you did only wake up a few hours ago, Jellybean."

"I know, I didn't sleep well, alright?" A bit of sharpness seeped into my tone, and I recoiled. I was tired, but I wasn't going to take it out on everyone. "Sorry, I just-"

"That's okay sweetie, you get your rest. Your father and I were about to take the kids down to Grans' to play." She elbowed my dad, trying to be sneaky, but I was sure that the whole world could see that jab.

"Ow- uhm, yes, we were." My dad grinned stupidly at me, then at my mom. "Have a nice nap." My parents hooked arms and walked out the door, calling, "Love you!"

I blew a kiss, then somehow found the energy to sprint to my room. I sunk like a rock into the plushy bed and instantly crashed into a lifeless sleep.

Spirit War

Chapter 2. Dreams and Gran

Call me weird if you like, but there was always this part of me that thought dreams were fascinating things, spinning your mind just when you thought you were dead to the world.

But this, this was something different. It wasn't a dream at all, it was a vision, curling with ugly reality and hissing with things you weren't scared of before, but were now.

It started out with nothingness, just pitch black and fuzzy. The darkness was thick, tangible almost, and as I waded through it, I saw something. A glimmer in the dark.

Fire.

It was the smallest of small, but the amount of potential was unforgiving. The flames looked me straight in the eyes, its unwavering confidence making me feel like the small one.

The fire had soon expanded to an average campfire size, and I could feel my hands sweating as it grew. And for the first time, I saw it.

The glimmering, burning, beautiful thing was hungry.

For destruction.

For damage.

For life.

And to me, it was alive as it shone and grew taller than me, till it was the only thing, the tallest, most confident thing ever made.

Oh no, oh no, here came the wind. It was a torpedo, whirling through the inky air towards me inevitably. I couldn't believe that we, in fact, represented the wind element and that we honored it every day.

I think I'll hate wind forever.

It made the fire so much worse, setting it into a frenzy and somehow stretching the wall of flames higher into the sky. The fire and wind launched into a horrific waltz, multiplying by the second.

Cue the water. It came out of the blackness, crashing and booming with authority but coolness. You'd think it'd join the battle, but rather it flowed out of its way to ignore it.

Instead of working hard, it worked smart. The slick water dug up the haunted pasts and found the toughest secrets. Then it seeped like guilt into the cracks you thought were sealed long ago. And that woke the earth.

It was rumbling and deep with not much to say and not very bright. But it was strong, powerful and loyal. It sent questionable cracks beneath me. Suddenly, I fell into them, my lungs vibrating with blood curdling screams.

My eyes flashed open, and I was panting hard. By far, that was the worst dream I'd ever had. Most of the time, I could kind of understand what the dream meant. Once, after I saw a giant spider on a hike, I dreamed about the gross thing the following night.

But I had no idea what this one meant. Noticeably, it had all the elements in it, but what could that mean?

Probably it meant that I was buying into Monnie and Luna's stories WAY too much, I thought and tried to roll my eyes. *Or I was overthinking fantasy legends.*

I sat up groggily, slowly adjusting and repeating "it was just a dream" like a chant in my head.

I glanced out the window and instantly realized it was darker than it should have been. Gosh, how long did I sleep for?

The weather had also shifted. Small drops of curious rain freckled my window, trees swaying slightly in the background. I hoped the fuzzy darkness was because of the rain and not the time, because if it wasn't, that'd be embarrassing. Sleeping the whole day. Ugh.

Still groggy, I tried my best to freshen up. But with my uneven hair, swollen-with-sleep face, and wrinkled clothes, it was nearly impossible. I brushed out my thick black hair, changed, and then stared at my helplessly puffy cheeks that held my weird gold eyes.

Oh well. I clambered out of my room, and instantly I knew it was too quiet. *They must still be at Grans',* I realized. My grandmother lived exactly a block away, in an adorable shabby house I knew so well — which I was headed to, until I saw that the sprinkling rain had become a reckless storm. Angry clouds, the tormented lightning strikes complimenting the booming thunder.

I ran for it. The gravel sidewalk hurt my feet and the rain slammed my back, but I made it to my grandmother's quickly although I was soaked. Right as I entered, warm, grandma-y scents smacked me in the face along with the twinkly laughter that belonged to Monnie, Luna and Atticus.

Baking cookies. Very strong raspberry perfume.

It was too intoxicating for my poor nose to handle. I sprinted for my grandma and hugged her like nothing else mattered.

"Bee! Oh, hello my darling!" Gran cooed enthusiastically.

"Hi, Gran." I watched all the creases in her face multiply as she smiled gently, her spacious, brown-red eyes twinkling with endless knowledge. "I smell cookies," I said pointedly, smirking. My mom had been encouraging more exercise and less sweets for my gran, but she hasn't been much about that.

"The whole folk won't let me stop, they need me to feed 'em," she would reply to my mom's critique, grinning like a child would. "They sure do love my cookin'."

There was nothing to say to that without lying. No one could resist the irresistible.

Anyway, my gran shot me a wink. "The cookies are for the kids, of course," she sniffed. "They wanted 'em. But maybe if there's leftovers . . ."

A high-pitched giggle slipped through my lips. Though my gran was ages older than me, sometimes she felt like the fun, slightly scandalous older sister I never had.

I mean, I had Eleanor, but that . . . Well, that was different.

Gran slipped her fingers into mine and we walked into the living room where the rest of my family was. "Look who's up!" My dad boomed, chortling with laughter. "Morning, Bee-Bee. Or should I say evening?"

"What time is it?" I replied instantly, freaking out. This was exactly what I didn't want.

"Four." My mom said carefully, seeing my face. "Is that alright?" How come moms always know something's wrong?

"Yeah, sorry, just trying to figure out why I slept so long . . ." I sighed and shook my head, cross with myself.

"Well, are you feeling okay? Sick or anything? Feverish?"

At the word sick, Gran rushed into the room from the kitchen, her forehead more creased than normal, ready to help. "You need cough drops? Aspirin?"

Warmed by their sympathy, I told them, "Nah, I feel perfect." And surprisingly, that wasn't a lie at all. Maybe it was the "nap" or maybe it was my loving Gran, but all those awkward feelings had disappeared.

In fact, I was feeling so perfect that the weather had surrendered to my happiness. I spotted the sun shyly peeking from behind a cloud. "Look, the rain's stopped," I informed everyone.

"Does that mean we can play outside?" Monnie asked giddily.

"Puh-LEASE?" Luna begged, her chocolate eyes dancing with excitement.

"Yeah, go for it kiddos," my dad smiled widely at their adorable eagerness. "Gran, would you take them to the park? It'll be a little slippery so I don't want them to go alone."

"Yay, Gran!" Monnie and Luna squealed. They'd found another victim of their play. What Gran didn't know was that she'd now be playing for all eternity.

"'Course, sugar," replied Gran, her lips curling scandalously. "Would you be a dear and just take out the cookies when the timer rings?" Of course, Gran knew just how much my dad was a flop with anything that involved baking and she liked to playfully tease him about it. I mean, don't masters get bragging rights?

I snickered and waited giddily to see my dad's humbling, humiliating "I-I would but, uhm, you know I don't really . . . bake."

The room erupted into laughter, and my dad, who was usually so gruff and tough, blushed bashfully. My mom grinned. "Aw, Gran, don't make fun of my poor little hubby," my mom cooed playfully, calling my dad by his nickname.

"Yeah, you better not," my dad said sniffly, trying but failing to caress a smile from his face. A jingly giggle escaped from my lips, unable to hold back in any way at all.

"And this is the part where they kiss," Gran shook her head, but her voice was sugary and her mahogany eyes glistened. I imagined her dredging up charismatic memories of them, pulling the cherished images from her huge, overflowing closet of endless echoes, the things that happened long ago.

"Ugh, grown-ups take forever." Rolling her chocolate eyes, Lunas' perfectly crafted face scrunched up. Everyone laughed at her little outburst, even Monnie, although she agreed. Honestly, I did too sometimes.

"I'll come outside also," I said.

"'Okay, sugar," Gran beamed and hugged me close. "Let's go, girls."

Chapter 3. The New Kid

It was still smothering, gross, and hot out. The many trees that surrounded us seemed to be trying to help, but I couldn't tell if they were doing anything.

"Good golly, it's hot out," coughed Gran, replaying my thoughts exactly. Monnie and Luna whined behind her, slowly trailing farther and farther behind.

"I'm going to go to the creek instead of the park," I decided and told our crew, pleased by the idea. Though it was slightly farther, I was practically salivating for the cool, rushing water and spongy moss.

"Okay, bye Blair!" my little sisters called. I broke off from the group and began to jog slightly. I wasn't paying full attention to where I was going, but my internal instinct was. So were my feet. The ground was damp with rain beneath them, squishy but refreshing.

Carefully, I started down the slope that led to the creek. I'd walked on the path so many times that the ivy that used to be there had disappeared; all that was left was dirt and some rocks. The terrain beneath me was slicker than usual, so it took me slightly longer, but I climbed down swiftly.

This was my haven. The cool water swept across my bare feet, soothing my every nerve. I clambered onto my favorite rock, a big, flat, and elephant-colored one. It was so perfectly positioned, catching half sun and half shade. Plus, a thin layer of clear water ran over it. Like I said, perfect.

I felt my eyes drooping, but I didn't want to resist. Relaxed, I closed my eyes and my breathing eased.

A smooth voice woke me. I jumped up, very alert. "Taking a snooze?" it said.

My brain assessed the voice. Young male sounding. But I had no idea who.

Like a slingshot, I yanked upward. Embarrassing, I thought-grumbled. Very embarrassing. It's always embarrassing when someone sees you sleeping—but a stranger? That was too much.

I didn't get a good look at him, my vision blurred with embarrassment and annoyance. Something about the boy antagonized me. "Yes," I cautioned. "A nap. Is that a problem?"

"Not at all," the boy replied coolly, spiking my annoyance. "A nice spot you have here." I focused harder on him, and really saw the boy for the first time. He looked my age, more or less. A mop of sandy blonde, curly hair topped his head that held bright blue eyes, baby pink cheeks and pearly skin.

"How old are you?" I spurted randomly. I had an urge to know. "Where are you from? And how come I've never seen you-"

"Enough with the questions," the boy snorted. Why was he so annoying? I just met him and he was interrupting me. "My name's Hudson Ignis. I'm thirteen but I'll be fourteen in a month. I just moved from Maine." Then he smiled in a torturously angelic way. "And you?"

"Blair, Blair Norwillo," I huffed, distracted, because nothing he said seemed to make sense. Why would he move from Maine? That was so far. Suspicious, I pried for more information. "So, whose house did you move into? I didn't know one was for sale."

Hudson shrugged, his dirty blonde curls bouncing from the motion. "The street over from here, not sure you'd know who-"

"Please, I know everyone," I cut in, boasting. "Benefits of a small town, you know?"

Hudson smirked. Pleased by the silent, unsaid challenge. "Ah, of course," he said sweetly. "His name was Aja."

"Hmm, the town crazy man," I said thoughtfully. Smiling smugly. "Always traveling. A bit . . . odd."

"Interesting," cooed Hudson. His perfectly arched eyebrow slowly raised upward. "Is his house haunted, then? Should I go fetch a nightlight?"

I tried to stay stone faced and cool. I wanted to roll my eyes indifferently but my lips . . . they curled rebelliously. A soft laugh billowed from my betraying vocal cords. "Dang you," I grumbled automatically, hopping athletically off from my elephant rock to where Hudson was standing. He laughed too, a sweet, smug sound.

"I really can't help it," Hudson said innocently. Almost . . . charismatic.

Okay, nuh-uh. I thought, disgusted. He was a stranger, an annoying stranger at most. Heat flooded my cheeks. What were we doing, just standing around?

I was the flash as I leaped back to my rock, forgetting about the wet ground. My foot slipped as I pushed off, catapulting me right into the creek. Shock froze me to the water. Right on my bum, I sat, the water laughing at me and splashing.

Hudson joined right in. His lips sprouted into an impish smile.

"Oh, just great." I pouted. Even my shadow was laughing, stretching up and down, coordinating with the sun. I was now soaking. Mini tadpoles darted away from me; just a giant, scary intruder.

"At least you're cooled down now," Hudson said in his sugary, innocent voice that was just too perfect. He leaped towards me still grinning in his devilishly angelic way. His legs stretched out as he jumped and then . . . splash! Hudson joined me in the water.

This time I didn't even try to hold back my laughter, chortling, loud and teasing. I mimicked him; "At least you're cooled down now."

He shrugged in response, tiredly smiling. His Caribbean Sea colored eyes glowed with warmth and not swag . . . and the tiny bits of surprise and decency etched into his pearl-colored features was calming.

I didn't lie to myself. Maybe, just maybe, I liked this little part of Hudson. Decent, warm, funny. Not like it was out often, though.

Soon, his mouth was twitching back into his trademark smirk. "I guess I've had a taste of my own medicine, now haven't I?"

I pursed my lips definitely. "Perhaps." Weirdly enough, we were both laughing. It felt odd to laugh with someone you didn't know, and who was so smug. But it felt good. Weird but good.

We sat in the creek for a while, a silence floating above our heads. But it wasn't uncomfortable, it just took awareness to balance everything. Looking up, smiling, eye-rolling and sighs. We splashed each other, and when Hudson got me right in the eye, my annoyance jumped.

From under my lashes I studied him again. In the sun, his skin was so pale it was the color of milk. He would undoubtedly stand out of here, as all of us were tanned from the sun. He also had a head of blonde, perfect ringlets and aqua-marine eyes, when all of us had dark eyes and straight hair.

But he had a compelling sense to him. I just wasn't sure if I liked it or not yet.

I sighed deeply, inhaling the sweet dew drop scent around me. The trees whispered around us, bushes crackling. One crackled louder than the others, though, loud and harsh. The sound made us both jump, our mouths shrink into little o's, our eyebrows bolted upright so high they touched our hairlines.

I thought maybe it was a fox or beaver, though both were rare to be seen near people. But I was more surprised with what I saw.

Who I saw, actually.

"Gran!" I yelped. "Hi." That was all I could say, hi. I ignored Hudson behind me completely; he wasn't even there at all anymore . . . although, I felt the pierce of his teal eyes boring into my back.

All I could see was Gran's wrinkled face popping from the bushes, a swirl of confusion and surprise bright in her deep, warm eyes. But there was knowledge permanently set in those eyes, and I knew she got the gist.

Nothing better than your grandma catching you with a boy, am I right?

"Gran," I said slowly. "This is Hudson, he's my age, he just moved into Aja's old house, we randomly just met." I held my breath, knowing that sentence was way too long.

Gran contorted her face, silvery eyebrows raised. "And you're sitting in the creek, all wet . . . because?" she prompted. For the first time, I whipped a glance at Hudson. He stood politely straight, his hands calmly by his sides. He seemed different than before, so obedient and respectful. But that sugary innocence was still there.

I bit my lip and tried to mirror his attitude. "Because . . . we fell in?" Of course, I failed. My voice hitched at the end of my sentence, like I was asking if it was an acceptable answer. Because honestly, it didn't seem like one.

"I'm sorry, ma'am," Hudson said, very deep and clear, speaking precisely. Had he been rehearsing this in his head the whole time? "I didn't mean to keep Blair at all. Just thought it'd be nice to make a friend in the neighborhood, you know?" His eyes gleamed.

Now, that was dirty. Guilt-tripping the elderly? Of course, though, Gran wasn't stupid.

"Right, right," she replied, shrugging. It might have been weird for any other grandma to shrug, but not my Gran. Her metallic hair strands waved as she followed through with the motion.

"Well, we just got worried, you were gone for quite a while!"

"We were?" I said stupidly, feeling waves of awkwardness overcome my coppery colored cheeks.

"An hour."

Hudson ripped his head toward his watch, and I felt relief overcome me for two reasons. One, he'd broken his 'So Perfect it's Scary' attitude and showed a glimpse of his real self. Two, at least he agreed it hadn't seemed like more than fifteen minutes either.

His voice was slightly off, even confused, as he complied, "She's right." In a cool manner, he tucked one of his loose, sunny ringlets behind his ear. It was just long enough that it stayed in place.

I swallowed, swatting away the millions of questions now buzzing around my head. It was like time had sped up and slowed at the same time, giving the world a buttery quality.

"Okay, I'm sorry." Sometimes a good sorry was all it took. "We just lost track of time."

Hudson nodded solemnly, and I felt proud of my clear voice and eye contact. But two seconds later, he smirked and dashed into the underbrush. His grin teased, *ha, good luck with your angry grandma,* but his eyes asked, *see you soon?*

I shot an upturned eyebrow that I hope screamed, *maybe, don't know and don't care,* as he disappeared. I still couldn't help thinking that I was lying a teensy bit. I wanted to see Hudson again. I just had to . . . think about things.

As soon as he disappeared, things sped up. I barely caught the suspicion flash in Gran's eyes, and things blurred in certain spots, like a low-quality photo.

I stared at Gran, and she stared at me right back, things becoming awkward. Finally, her crackly but singsong voice shattered the silence. "We better check on the little girls."

Chapter 4. A Visitor

You're probably thinking, *well, at least she's with her fun, rebellious grandma and not her "no boys rule" parents, right?*
WRONG.
You don't know how much I'd give to be with anyone but Gran. She seemed changed, if that could possibly happen in one hour. Her usually smiling lips were tightened into a straight line, her care-free, jolly brown eyes were not so jolly right now.

She kept sneaking glances at me, which was odd too. Gran was more a "do it or don't" person. There was no in between glances! There was also something deep in her eyes that was rare . . . Worry?

Fear?

I hoped it was the first option. Worry made sense. I mean, any grandma would worry when her granddaughter started hanging out with her first boy friend. (Not boyfriend, to be clear! Two totally separate words).

Hudson doesn't even like me, I thought-grumbled. My mind flashed to his teal eyes and bouncy blonde curl tucked behind his pearly colored ear. His winning smirk, and his playful water splashes. *And I don't like him either,* I huffed.

A part of me just had to keep going.

We're actually not friends either, I countered, *and we weren't "hanging out".* *We didn't MEAN to meet up, anyway.* I rolled my eyes, but then, *why was Gran worried?*

I glared at my reflection in the calm creek, and it glared right back. I hated that I was the cause of my own grandma's anxiety, worry, and possibly fear.

The thing though, about my reflection, was that the most intriguing thing was my eyes, and not the withering glaring shooting from them. They were bright in contrast to the dark, smooth rocks and fuzzy, pine green moss. The bright gold, shimmering, unique things that were part of me didn't seem to match my dark, frizzy hair and average tan face. People around here complimented them often, which was sort of embarrassing. But the look in their eyes was worse; an expectancy, almost, or an accusation.

I shivered, though it was a million degrees. Gran grabbed my hand and squeezed it, but still didn't look at me. Yet the motion got my heart beating again. It was the kind of thing that said, I'm not mad, we just have to talk.

That was a good start.

I really wasn't paying attention to where we were walking, so I was more than surprised when we ended up in Gran's driveway.

"You said we were checking on Monnie and Luna, at the park!"

Gran chuckled, and sweet bliss rolled through me at the sound. "Old minds like mine can never keep up with this new generation, now can they?" This time she faced me completely, and I looked up at her smile. It's back! I almost cheered, then stopped because I saw just a teensy bit of something in her sunny eyes. A suspicious little cloud that at any moment, had the potential of a storm.

"I meant to tell you I already dropped them off with your mama and dada. Of course, it slipped my mind," Gran shook her head tiredly.

So then checking on the girls must have been an excuse to leave, I guess. And it had slipped her mind to tell me because she was too busy worrying.

"I'm sorry, Gran!" I cried, all the words I wanted to say piling up. "I don't know why, but I know I'm worrying you! Is it because of Hudson? I promise I've never seen him before in my life except for now! He's annoying, too, so we're not friends at all. Please Gran, stop worrying, pretend none of this ever happened!" I took a breath. It was shaky as I waited for her response.

The response was, surprisingly, a hug.

And it felt amazing.

This hug nurtured apology, love and relief. It may have been hot, but now it was the perfect temperature. I fit into Gran's curves and edges the two matching puzzle pieces would. A little wet spot pooled on my cheek as we pulled away.

"Oh, Bee-Bee don't cry, my darling. You'll make me cry and then . . ." Her finger traced my cheek. "Emotions are just running high right now. Especially for you."

I smiled though I didn't understand. *Especially for me?* What did that mean?

We climbed the many stairs then entered Gran's grand house. Like ours, it was spirally, tall, and a faded gray color. The landscaping was worse, though. It was just dirt. The sidewalk, which was barely even there anymore, had almost caused several broken body parts.

We came through the door and immediately heard twinkly cheers of excitement that obviously belonged to my little siblings. I frowned, confused.

We came into the big common room where my parents sat anxiously on the tattered couch, but they had planted a seed of a fake smile on both their faces. Monnie and Luna danced around happily while Atticus tried to join, but failed on his wobbly legs.

As soon as my mom and dad spotted me, they rushed up and pulled me into a slightly violent hug.

"What's going on?" I said, or at least tried to say because I was getting absolutely smothered. It ended up as, "Phats goin m?"

"Jellybean, you were gone for hours," my dad said deeply, his forehead crinkled with little worry lines.

"But Gran told me it was just an hour-" I started to say, but my mom cut in. Her voice was surprisingly soft and gentle.

"Multiple hours, actually." Mama pushed, and Gran raised a finger to her lips slyly. "And for the other big news, Blair. . . What Monnie and Luna were excited about . . ." My heart thundered in my chest. When moms were this careful and gentle, it was never good. "Well, don't take this the wrong way but . . ."

"Ellie's coming to visit!" squealed Monnie.

"All the way from her big new house." Luna smiled. I couldn't help thinking how innocent she looked.

"You mean her school, Luna," I said, choking over my own tongue. My voice was raw as I turned to my parents. "Eleanor is coming to visit from her boarding school?" I could never say her name casually ever again. She would never be Ellie again.

"Well," my dad swallowed. "We didn't-"

"After all this time!?" I shrieked, suddenly enraged. "She thinks she can just march up here after she's been totally ignoring every single one of us!? SHE THINKS-"

"Ellie!" laughed Atticus cheerfully. "Ellie, Ellie, Ellie," he said her name, throwing it around happily. The name of my one older sister. The one who ghosted us all.

Chapter 5. Remembering

Tears sprang in my eyes and quickly I tried to make them vaporize. One of the worst things to ever do is cry when you're hurt but not by a cut or scrape, by words. Especially when you're also fighting with that person.

Gran placed a weathered hand on my shoulder. "Honey, they haven't even asked her yet," she whispered.

I glanced up blankly. "Wait, you haven't?"

"Actually, no," Mama cautioned. "But Bee-Bee, I wanted you to be prepared. She will want to come down."

I snorted, getting flashbacks of the time I tried to call or text, or ask her to come visit. "What in your right mind," I began, rolling my eyes hugely, "makes you think that she will randomly be like, 'sure, I'll come down and visit y'all!' After all those tries? What changed?" I huffed.

No response, of course. There was sympathy in all the adults' eyes, but also an icy hardness.

"Blair," Gran said.

"Yes?"

"Has it been hot lately?" Gran asked.

I frowned, feeling interrogated. "Very hot. Why?"

"Have you been feeling . . . tired, lately?" She continued her weird questions. "Been getting weird dreams, too?"

I froze. Gran knew? No, she couldn't know. But then why . . . My thoughts buzzed and I swallowed hard. "I don't know." My voice shook with the weight of the white lie. Three words, and it was that hard.

"Blair, now's an important time," pointed out my mom. "It would be a bad idea to lie."

"Hey, you think I'm lying?" I said sadly, thinking how Luna and Hudson were both flawlessly innocent. I tried to mimic them. I think I was failing, because instead of softening her features, she just shrugged.

"I didn't say you were," My mom started, but my dad grinned in a sad way.

"Let's just say," he chuckled breathily, "that you're not the best liar."

"Okay, that too," my mom caved, making Gran smirk. I sighed and rolled my eyes.

"But in all seriousness, Blair, you have to remember she's still your sister. Your older sister, in fact. Going to a far away boarding school for high school all alone is a big thing to do considering she's only fourteen. There's a lot she's been dealing with. You have to understand that."

I shook my head. "Doesn't anyone here see that it was *her* choice to leave us? That she chose not to answer any calls or texts!" I took a big breath and continued, though I knew it was a bad idea just by a glance at both my parents' faces. "Doesn't anyone see that she WOULDN'T LET US VISIT HER ON VISITING DAY!?"

"That's enough, Blair," Dada said. Tears started running down my cheeks. He pulled me onto his lap that I was too big for. "Honey, I know you two were very close, and that she was your role model. That makes it harder to forgive her for leaving."

I sniffled. Mama scooted closer to me on Dada's lap. Gran walked over to where we were sitting on her tattered brown couch with my favorite gold tassels. They matched my eyes . . . And Eleanor's, now that I'm thinking about her.

My mind flashed to when I last saw her. She had creamy warm skin and glossy black hair. She had a bouncy, sweet smile that reached up high in her rosy cheeks. But the day she left she wasn't wearing it; only a stern line etched into her face.

Plus, her eyes that were a breathtaking gold (hundreds of times better than mine) were hidden by an ugly, muddy colored brown contacts. She was the one person in my family who shared my eyes and they were always a special thing between us. The fact she was covering them hurt more than anything.

Eleanor was wearing her boarding school uniform when she left. It was a classic uniform — plaid skirt and a white, button-up top. She also wore a milk chocolate colored blazer that matched her skirt, with a fancy little pin that clasped onto it.

Eleanor was so beautiful in that uniform, I remembered. We waited at the bus stop with her even though she was moody and didn't want us there at all. Mama was tearing up and Dada was shaking with silent sobs.

Then the bus pulled up, slow and calm. It didn't match my racing heartbeat, and it looked evil with its pointed headlights and thick windshield wipers. The little bus was pristine and white with one sky blue stripe down the middle. In neat printing on top of the blue line, it said the name of the school, Birming Dale High, School of Arts.

Mama kissed her goodbye, while Monnie, Luna and Atticus sobbed. Eleanor's blush was clearly visible despite her bronze skin. She gave one practiced wave and got into the bus without looking back.

I remember my chest hurt from silent weeps. My gold eyes were glassy. I didn't want to be sad at all, but sometimes you can't avoid it. Dada pulled me in, and his earthy scent flooded my nose.

"Ellie's where she needs to be," Dada said, and I had stared at him confusedly in return. "She needs to figure things out, Bee-Bee. But I know she'll be back. To help you."

With what? I realized it now. Was she coming to help me? Was that what Mama had meant when she said Eleanor would want to come down? I sighed. But with what, exactly? I rolled my eyes.

Soon it was dinner time. All I wanted was to be alone with my thoughts. There was so much going on, I just wanted to think. Even Gran's cooking couldn't soothe my nerves, the juicy, seasoned steak and hearty broccoli.

I was quiet all night, but no one pressed me about it. Gratitude for them swept through me. Although I was surprised and anxious, I knew I was lucky to have them all here for me.

I lay in my bed late that night. I didn't want to go to sleep and dream vividly weird, element-y dreams I knew were warning me. From what, I didn't know. Of course, though, I couldn't stay up the whole night worrying. I had to be ready for whatever challenges tomorrow would bring . . . Eleanor, Hudson, Gran?

I gulped and knew I had to eventually face the dreams. They were always waiting in the corners of my mind . . . I closed my eyes and met them.

Chapter 6. I Hate Dreams

I was in a vivid, so-colorful-it-hurts field. Everything sparkled and smelled a little too much like that artificial strawberry scent. Fluffy rainbows danced in the sky, and the grass was a neon green. Uncontrollably, my mouth stretched into a wide grin, and weirdly enough, I didn't feel my two front teeth. I wiggled my tongue into the crooked gap, feeling six again.

That was when I saw the smoke. It was gray, thick and ugly, rising higher and higher in the sky. My heart hammered against my rib cage, and I was sure it would crack. It felt like something bad was about to happen . . .

Just a dream, just a dream, I tried to think, but it felt like a prison, trapping me in until I got the lesson.

The air clumped up with humidity and the scent of fire. I yelled as the ground trembled, stitch by stitch ripping apart.

And then I fell.

I tumbled down, the air screaming in my ears, whistling by me insanely fast. I flipped multiple times as the ground zoomed closer, making me feel faint. I fell so fast I couldn't blink or move my mouth to scream. All I could do was brace mentally for the fall as the dark brown, cracking ground whizzed way too close.

But then . . . I didn't smash into itty bitty pieces.

I sucked in a huge breath, shaking with adrenaline. I wasn't dead. I wasn't dead! Instead, I floated several inches above the ground. I don't know how, because I couldn't see any part of my body but I wasn't dead.

I wasn't dead.

After that sank in, I felt glorious. Around me, it smelled like sharp, clear, wind. The breeze pulsed with power, lifting me higher above the mud, dirt and cracked ground. It was nothing more than a loyal servant while I was the queen.

I smiled and quickly zoomed higher. Flying is fun, I thought blissfully. Wind rushed behind me so slowly, while I was a cheetah.

And then, suddenly, I fell. I screamed so loud it hurt my throat, and I hideously tumbled down to the horrendous ground.

I woke up with clammy hands and my brown frizzy hair stuck to my forehead. It was just a dream! I reprimanded myself, but a dream had never felt this real before. And I could control it, weirdly enough. I was never in control of my dreams before.

My stomach dropped. Before what? I wondered, shivering as I

threw off my blanket and got up. Outside, it was gloomy and dark, so I had no idea what time it was. The rain made soothing, repetitive taps on my windowsill, and I could very faintly hear croaks of the toads at the creek. The sounds begged me for more sleep, but I resisted.

Atticus was the only one of my other siblings who was awake, and he cooed and shrieked and occasionally babbled things very close to words. My dad sat with him on the floor, talking in a blissfully cheery and high voice that was rare nowadays.

The sight was comforting, and I almost wanted to stay there for hours just watching them. But I kneeled down and said hi.

"Hey buddy," I sang to Atticus, and a four toothed smile spread across his face. I hugged my dad, and warmth spread through me. Sometimes it felt like dads forgot about things that happened yesterday, which made them more lovable.

"Morning, Jellybean," he said, his sunny eyes seeming to light up the room.

"Morning," I replied. "Is Mama at work?"

"Mm-hm," Dada answered, turning back to Atticus and softly laughing. "Right, little man? And we're going to have lots of fun with daddy, right? Isn't that right!" His sugary, ecstatic voice made me playfully roll my eyes. I'd leave them to their guy talk.

Soon, Monnie and Luna woke up too and ate breakfast with me. They were groggy, and I was thinking, so we made a good match as we traded bits of conversation. Mostly, I thought about Eleanor coming, and when would she come, if she would, and all those technicalities. But also about Hudson. I wondered if he'd be at the creek in a little while. I wanted to go there after breakfast to check, but not just for him. I craved the fresh air and cool water.

So, when I finished my Corn Flakes, I announced to Monnie and Luna, "Want to come to the creek with me?" They nodded eagerly, and I glanced at Dada. "Can we?" I asked.

He bit his lip. Usually he wasn't this skeptical, but I knew why he was. "As long as you stick with Blair. It's also still raining slightly, so be very careful," he instructed, pointedly looking at me. I got a flashback of Hudson and me slipping into the creek. "Don't go too far, and only go in the shallow part-"

"We know, we know!" complained Monnie, sounding bored. "We went there yesterday, and the day before, and the day before that, and . . . and . . ." She trailed off.

"The day before that," Luna finished with satisfaction.

Dada smiled. "Alright, alright." But he still looked at me, a piercing look in his eyes. He tapped his wrist, right where a watch would lay. *Don't be late,* the action screamed. For what, I wasn't not sure.

But I knew I would not be late.

Chapter 7. No Sign of You-Know-Who

The weather was again, grossly hot. The slight rain that trickled down my back tried to cool the steaming world down, but the humidity clung to you hungrily, draining your life force like an evil wind spirit could do.

We walked on the gravel path for two blocks or so then turned left and went through the mangy brush that hid the 'path', which was just a space we'd walked on so much that the ivy and grass eroded away. Magnolia and Luna trailed behind me, splashing in every single puddle.

Once we got there, I played with Monnie and Luna, a game where we had magical powers that allowed us to talk to animals — but after a while, I just wanted to talk to . . . well, Hudson. They started to branch off anyway, trading words to only each other, eyes glinting with creativity in sync.

Of course, I kept a close eye on the sun to tell the time. It seemed like forever, waiting for Hudson, but we hadn't been there long at all. The scent of morning still lingered in the air, a mix of dew drops and bird tweets.

But still, every second sent the sun slightly higher in the air. I eyed Monnie and Luna, but they were fine. So I focused on the sun that sometimes hid behind those dark clouds in the air. *Okay, keep on going slow,* I begged silently. The longer we were here the better. Eventually, though, I sighed and got up in a sluggish way. My limbs felt glued to my cozy, cool, elephant rock. I shook it off.

"Okay, girls, let's head back now." A teensy part of me felt proud of the authority in my voice, the planning ahead I was doing. *Dada will be pleased,* I smiled, happy. But then, my mind just had to float to the problems that awaited me deep in the corners of my mind.

Eleanor and Hudson. Gran? I didn't want to think about Gran.

But Eleanor. I focused on her. Maybe she'd be the same. But what if she was changed? Fear coursed through my bones, but I snorted. *Of course she'll be changed,* I inhaled shakily. *She's in high school now. She doesn't live here anymore. She's not Ellie.*

That was another thing. I overheard her telling Mama and Dada that Birming Dale High was a fresh start for her and all that stuff, so she wanted to be called Eleanor now, instead of Ellie. This hurt, to say the least. Ellie was what I called her, so often that sometimes I forgot her real name was actually Eleanor. It was so . . . her.

Until. She changed.

I called it The Change. Pretty self-explanatory. Something happened at a sketchy party, is all I know. There might've been fighting and bad people, but you didn't hear that from me — it was what Jess, the gossip girl and rumor spreader at my school told us.

I knew Mama and Dada didn't want Eleanor, Ellie at the time, to go to the party. How she begged and begged. I remember actually joining sides with her, convincing our parents it was just a silly eighth grade party.

Clearly, it wasn't.

But they caved.

Mama drove her out of our neighborhood to the borders of town. She dropped her at Campsite #13, she told us. *"Bad luck, and I knew it,"* Mama had bit her lip whenever retelling the lucid tale.

I went to bed that night, clueless and oblivious. I thought about Eleanor as I dozed off, missing her in the bed next to me. We had shared a room back then.

But when I woke up, I was met with a note that held shaky writing.

Blair-

Gone with Eleanor. Trouble at the party last night. Please watch the littles. Be back by 10.

XOXO, Mama and Dada

I didn't not worry. But I didn't think it was so serious. That one, vague note would change my life. I sighed heavily, feeling a burn inside me. Why was I antagonizing myself like this? I thought about it. To prepare, I decided.

Sure enough, when I got back, Dada was waiting for me at the door. I felt like he was about to break bad news and considering all circumstances, he probably was.

"Nice job, Blair. They behaved?" He asked, stone-faced. I knew he was trying not to give anything away, but I knew Dada too well. Anyway, he sucked at lying. Here's why — whenever he lied, or was worried, he talked in short sentences. He also tried to make it seem like he wasn't lying by being all cool, but that didn't work either. It seemed like everything he did highlighted the bad news rather than hid it . . . But maybe I was being self-conscious?

Dada ruffled Luna and Monnie's hair, which made Luna giggle and Monnie exclaim, "Don't mess my hair up!"

Dada laughed his throaty, addictive laugh and I started to relax. "Sorry, kiddo," he nudged Monnie. I started to smile, but then saw Gran. Normally, I would have instantly grinned my face off, but by her expression, she looked grim. It seemed like she was almost hiding, kind of standing behind Dada. Her forehead was more creased than normal, making the worry lines stand out. Her silvery eyebrows knit together, like Mama's did sometimes.

Yet, as soon as she caught me staring at her, she stepped from behind Dada and held her arms out. She smiled, but her eyes were dull and unfocused, like she was really someplace far away. I knew as soon as I saw that her cloudy brown eyes that were usually sunny, that she was having one of her Bad Days.

Dada seemed to read my thoughts. "Gran's having a hard day," he frowned. His words were careful and sympathetic like always, but today a worried and slightly hard edge crept into them. I felt Dada glance at me, but I didn't look back. What was going on?

Gran having Bad Days was not uncommon. She had them about once a month. They always scared me, those cloudy, muddled eyes staring into nothingness . . . It seemed like she was half-dead sometimes. Once, she stayed in her room the whole day. I know my parents sometimes try to hide it by saying she's had a hard day or she's sick, or she has an awful headache, but I just call it her Bad Days. The only thing reassuring about them is that Gran always comes back, better than ever.

"What's going on?" I said, trying to keep the fear and confusion out of my voice. I wanted to sound bossy, confident, smug . . . just like Hudson.

Dada placed a hand on my shoulder. It felt warm but heavy. Solid.

"Well, we were going to wait until Mama came back from work." I saw in his eyes; he was just as scared as I was. Oh no, I knew what was coming. "But . . . It's confirmed, Blair. Eleanor is coming to visit."

Chapter 8. Dragons

Why now? Why after all this time?

That was what I really wanted to ask. Instead, I swallowed, trying to keep cool. "When?"

Dada squirmed. He didn't like being under pressure. He liked brief sentences and brief answers. "Ellie— I mean, Eleanor," he began, "is coming tomorrow morning."

My insides lurched. That was so soon. When I woke up, Eleanor would be sleeping beside me like before. I would have to sneak from my— I mean, *our* bedroom to not wake her up. She hated waking up early like I do. Excuses buzzed through my brain.

"School," I said, panting a little. "School starts tomorrow. She can't come," I said, faking sympathy, but bitterness crept in. "We'll have to cancel." Dada looked at me sternly. A little guilt crept into me. She's still my sister . . . But the hurt came crashing back. She left. She ghosted us. Right?

The thing is, it doesn't seem like Elli- Eleanor at all to do such a thing. Then again, she changed.

Dada pursed his lips. His warm brown eyes screamed, don't push it! "There's a heat advisory warning," he explained. "The whole Woodland County is shutting down for an extra week. Anyway, we always put family first; you know that."

"Right." Sarcasm climbed into my voice. "Clearly, Eleanor *always* puts *us* first. Being family and all."

The sparks in Dada's eyes burst and ignited. "Blair." The anger in his voice was crystal clear, and constantly amplifying. "You don't know what she's going through!" He barked, causing me to flinch, but he kept going. "She's your sister. Treat her like one." Dada's bushy black hair and big hands shook with withering anger.

Tears welled up in my eyes, the whole world tilting and swinging, blurring up at the edges. It felt like I was centering on something deep inside me, pulling from an emotional reserve I never knew I had. Steaming anger, storms of fear, mountains of guilt and firing hatred. It was a volcano that had been building up for a long time.

I ran outside before it could erupt.

It was raining much harder now. Thunder boomed in the distance, rattling the ground slightly. Lightning gleamed like thousands of spiky knives. Perfect weather to match the perfect mood.

I let out a shuddery breath. Sprinting through the grass and gravel roads, I was silently crying. Uncontrollable sobs escaped my lips, and I didn't hold back at all. There was something shifting inside me and I was embracing it.

Nothing mattered anymore.

All I wanted was the creek. I envisioned it so clearly in my head. The vibrant trees smiling pleasantly, small pebbles and sand sifting through your toes, and the big, mossy rocks that the water slid over.

'O wind gods, help me. I found prayers popping up in my head. Where were they coming from? *Mighty wind gods, hear this prayer.* It didn't sound like my voice.

I had made it to the creek. Water yanked me this way and that, but I held my ground. The current was much, much stronger than usual, spraying up and blending in with the tears running down my face. The prayers kept coming too, louder and louder. They started to make my headache, all those screaming little voices yelling prayers.

Help her, 'O powerful wind gods! One screamed. I crumpled to the ground yelling. My head pounded and my body crumpled to the water. *Stay calm, young one.* Another voice said. It sounded high and pinched.

The voices were of all kinds, old and young, female and male. So maybe that's why I heard a familiar voice in the mix. *Deep breaths, Blair,* it said. My heart practically stopped. Was that . . . Eleanor? No, it couldn't be. I had to be going mad!

You're not going crazy, Eleanor's voice said, like it was reading my mind. Actually, it probably was. Her voice was smooth with a hint of that big sister sass, just as I had remembered it. My skin tingled crazily. Then came an itching sensation. I screamed, and it sounded like it almost stretched into a mighty roar. *Almost there!* A voice soothed, too familiar. It wasn't Eleanor this time, instead . . . *You got this, Blair,* Hudson said. Again, my heart did something crazy. Instead of stopping, it sped up ten times faster than it was going before. The voices kept coming, but I channeled in on Hudson. You got this, Blair, he had said. I had to show him.

I got this!

That's when my feet slowly lifted off the ground. My arms . . . no, my wings were flapping majestically. Wings! I had wings. Sweet bliss rolled through me. I could also see a different view from each eye, like a horse could, or bird, or whale . . .

Or an animal.

Oh my spirits! I was an animal, an animal that could fly, nonetheless. I was huge too. The trees that surrounded the creek bent from just the weight of the air coming from my wings. I glanced downward to see gold, shimmering scales, and a thrashing, barbed tail.

No. Way! I was a dragon! A giggle escaped my lips, but it sounded like a snort. Because I was a dragon.

My gold scales seemed to shift in the light. They were so, so beautiful. The sun hit them in the perfect way, and they sent beams of yellow, vivid light everywhere. There were also scales that were tiny shades darker than the others, creating a pattern of intriguing swirls and lines.

And my senses! Oh, they were about millions of times better. I could see everything in perfect detail, the slightest dent in each thumb-nail sized rock, each individual grain of sand, the smooth edges on all the bright green leaves. The hearing and the smelling were better too; I could hear rushing water of the creek and the birds tweeting and someone's faint footsteps who was going for a walk. I smelled bark and fresh water, and also . . .

A boy?

Someone was watching me. I couldn't believe I hadn't been more careful! My heart seemed to tear a hole in my chest and beat right through it. My eyes darted around, trying to find who was peeping in on dragon-me. It was overwhelming, but eventually I found him. Or, his eyes.

The aqua marine eyes were the only things I could see of the boy, and I couldn't help but think; no one had blue eyes like that in our community except for . . . Hudson. The color of them was so painstakingly cute I would have screamed if I was in human form.

I snuffled in deep breaths, trying to calm down. *Maybe it's not Hudson.* I thought, but I knew it had to be. If it wasn't Hudson, whoever it was would be running away screaming instead of silently watching. Also, who else would be here, at the creek, in the same exact place as yesterday? *Okay, well, he doesn't know it's me.* Actually, that might have been false too. He could have been watching when I . . . transformed. But if he wasn't, then all I had to do was NOT transform back in front of him.

Then it hit me.

What if I couldn't turn back?

I'd be stuck as a dang dragon, that's what. My whole body started to quiver. No one would know who I was. I'd have to leave Mama and Dada and Gran and my little siblings . . . People would find out. Everyone would. I'd be dragged into a tortuous testing room — or worse, killed.

If dragons could cry, I'd be sobbing away.

Just go back to the way it was, I cried inwardly. *Everything was perfect then . . . Eleanor was Ellie, it was summer, there were no confusing boys . . .*

So much had happened in a month, and my brain didn't seem to want to process it. Or maybe I was just overwhelmed by all these amplified senses. My ears picked up on useless sounds I didn't want to hear. But maybe all of them weren't useless . . . because I could hear someone running my way — fast.

The footsteps were heavy on the gravel, and they made a harsh, crunching noise beneath them. As they drew closer, I smelled the sweat of an anxious person and the thick smell of a man. He was coming closer and closer.

What should I do? What should I do!? WHAT SHOULD I DO!?!

Thoughts like that ran through my head unbearably fast. But it was too late to really do anything. I heard the worried man come down the path and then . . . slowly, I turned around, (knocking off several tree branches in the process; the creek wasn't that wide). And then, I was met with . . .

Dada.

I had never been happier to see someone in my entire life. His frizzed black hair looked more puffed up than normal. He actually had a twig stuck in his big dark beard. Dada stood next to dragon-me, his firm build in a kind of defensive position.

My heart jumped. *Help, Dada,* I wanted to say. I don't think I've thought that in a while, and especially not said it. It felt good.

"Okay, Jellybean," Dada said, shaking. I noticed little green flecks in his shimmering brown eyes. I was so focused remembering each detail about him, I didn't realize that he had called me Jellybean. He knew who I was! I was so happy I didn't even question how he knew.

Yet maybe I was a little too excited, because I flapped my brilliant wings. They sent a powerful gust of air hurtling toward Dada. My heart broke as I saw him tumble to the ground, landing weirdly on his ankle. Dada grunted in pain, and I whined mournfully. *I'm so sorry, Dada.*

He got up, limping and rubbing his ankle. I could see the brave face he was putting on.

"I'm fine, Bee-Bee," said Dada gruffly, like he did whenever he got hurt. I hung my head and nuzzled it against him. He yelped, and I skittered back. "You've got no idea what you can do, Blair." He smiled, but his voice contained a twinge of mysteriousness. Dada then pointed to the top of my head. I couldn't see what he was pointing to though, and I tried to crane my neck in each way. This made him laugh his deep, throaty laugh I loved so much.

"Horns," he chuckled. "You've got horns, Jellybean." My breath quickened. I could tell he was having fun being the smart one while I was clueless. I slapped my tail against the water, sending a tsunami toward him. He jumped back. I snorted, like, *um, remember? A little help here!*

"Right, then," he said. Seriousness climbed its way back into his voice. "I've been told transforming back is not a pleasant experience, Blair." Jellybean was gone suddenly.

"The first time is always the hardest, though," he continued. "Now, just close your eyes." I did what he said, but I was terrified. "I want you to breathe with me. In, out, in, out." My breathing snuffled in sync to his words, though I didn't see how this would help.

"Relax all your muscles," he said. The voice he was using sounded like all the online workout instructors' voices, or maybe like Mama's yoga teacher. He looked at me. "Shifting is about truly facing your fears. That means, to cross between the reality and the spirit world, you must address why you transformed in the first place. Got it?"

I nodded, but I barely grasped a word he said. Perhaps if he knew so much about . . . Whatever this was, then he could change— or, Shift, as he'd called it, too.

Hope flared. Maybe I wasn't alone in this process.

"Go ahead, Blair," Dada said. I realized I had been keeping him waiting. My tail whisked behind me instinctively. Nervously. *I had to address why I transformed in the first place.* Out of all things, why that!? Right now, that was exactly the thing I wanted to block out.

But I wanted to Shift back to a human. Either way, the process wouldn't be fun, right? So . . .

I concentrated. It was mostly Eleanor. And a little bit of Gran and Hudson. Nerves flicked inside me, but nothing happened.

"You have to admit your mistake," Dada added helpfully. His voice was far away.

Ugh, I made such a big mistake when I got mad that Eleanor left us. I made such a big mistake accidentally bumping into the new kid and talking to him, I thought sarcastically. But I had to focus.

I shouldn't blame everything on Eleanor because she left. She was having trouble with things. I'm her sister, I should never give up on her.

I wanted to puke with guilt. My heartbeat felt so loud I'm sure Dada could hear it. I remembered the nights we'd sit and talk together for hours about anything at all. Her oversized pajamas she always wore, her glossy black hair slicked back into the crafty braid she slept in every night.

My body was shaking wildly; I could feel it now, vibrating uncontrollably.

Her gold eyes would glitter when she talked. One night, she told me all about middle school and how it goes. "You got this," she had said when I confided that I was nervous, smiling in that big sisterly way. But now she was gone, far, far away.

And I actually *wanted* her gone? I trembled at the malicious thought. *I'm sorry, Ellie, I want you to come home. Please, Ellie.*

Again, the voices started to flow through my head, but I couldn't pick them out. They were going a mile a minute. Then, they merged into a consistent annoying buzz in the corner of my brain, like a headache. My breath shuddered, and realized I was sobbing crazily.

That's when I realized; sobbing? Dragons couldn't cry.

I glanced at my hands and saw they were perfectly normal human hands. Then, I looked back up to Dada, standing a few feet away. He seemed insanely worried. As soon he saw I was okay, we ran toward each other, fast as bullets. He pulled me in a Papa-bear worthy hug, practically squeezing my life out.

It felt amazing.

Dada looked so sturdy standing there, but I knew we both felt the weight of what just happened. His big, blocky hands gripped my tangled hair, and I dangled about a foot above ground in his grasp.

"It's okay, Jellybean. Everything will be okay."

The words may not have been fully believable, but they were truly the best words I'd heard in a long time.

Chapter 9. A Bad Day

Gran was watching Monnie and Luna, but not really. Her eyes still were glazed over, hypnotized, but she seemed almost frustrated. Her wrinkled hand was clenched into a fist.

"Gran," Dada said, his voice ringing with exhaustion. He was still limping though, just barely. I said I was sorry three times already, and he'd shooed me off, but my stomach clenched with worry. I could say sorry a million times, yet I'd still feel awful about hurting my own father.

"It's okay, Gran. You can stop now," continued Dada, and he shook her bony shoulder.

This made her intake a sharp, startled, gasp. She was instantly broken from her spell, her eyes illuminating, her bronze-colored hand relaxed from the fist. It was reliving to see her back truly alive, but my jaw hung in the air, dropped down to my toes. I had never seen her become unhypnotized in real life before. Just one day she was there, the next day she wasn't.

"Blair . . .?" She looked horrified. My breathing stopped as I felt Dada nod behind me. "Oh, spirits, Blair!" cried Gran, pulling me towards her. I smelled her strawberry perfume flowing like a river into my nose. "You're so young, baby," Gran said; she was tearing up. "I'm sorry you had to go through with this," she added. "But you'll be proud, one day."

Confusion stirred inside me. "You . . . know what happened?" This brought me to another question, but this one was for Dada. "And how did YOU, Dada, know I was the—well, the . . ."

"Dragon?" finished Dada. Gran's expression was soft, sympathetic.

"Yeah."

I still didn't believe it — or even say the word aloud. I could turn into a dragon. It didn't make sense; you couldn't just turn into a dragon and poof, you were, but there were no other words. When I thought about it, it reminded me of . . .

"Oh!" I shouted, kind of excited. "It's like the legends."

"Yes," Gran confirmed in an astonished voice. "I'm surprised you figured it out, darling. Ellie didn't figure it out until the ritual." My heart gave a wild jump. I could have told her that I actually thought about the dragon stories often, but of course, I focused on the mention of Eleanor. Was she a dragon, too? It made my breath quicken, my body tingle . . .

Eleanor's' voice popped into my head. That was a bad sign. *Stop it,* she said, her voice fading. *Control yourself.* Eleanor sounded strained, her voice slightly shrilly.

It made me remember Visiting day. I was so, so, excited. I put on my favorite light blue jeans, the ones with the cool pockets on the sides and my gold sweater with the three buttons. The one that used to be Eleanor's, that she said complimented our eyes.

We drove all the way to Birming Dale High, which was a full hour away. It was a huge, stony school, tall as a skyscraper with towers that corkscrewed into the air. It looked a little like our house, just one hundred times bigger and grander. And it definitely didn't look like a cruddy high school that people complained about. No, it looked like it jumped out straight from a Harry Potter book.

We sat in the auditorium while the principal gave a super long speech. It was about supporting your child during hard times and braving the evil spirits, or something, but I wasn't paying much attention. I was too excited to see Ellie, and plus, the principal lady had the most boring voice in history. It was flat and emotionless, droning on and on.

If the principal lady had to deal with kids like Eleanor all day, I can't blame her for that gray, tired voice.

Finally, we were led into the gym, where a party was set up. There were colorful streamers, flashing lights and long tables with punch and chips. It was hands-down, the coolest party I'd ever been to, I had thought, and that's when the freshman started to pour in.

There were hugs and smiles everywhere, but no Eleanor. We searched the crowded, loud, gym, finally giving up and asking a teacher.

She was a plump, middle-aged woman with a smiley face and rosy cheeks. She wore a flowy dress printed with flowers, and teensy glasses too small for her wide eyes. It may have been the flashing lights, but I could've sworn her eyes were teal.

"Hello there, huns," she smiled, her mouth filled with big white teeth. I figured out quickly she loved saying hun.

"Hi," Mama had replied briskly, worried. "Do you know our daughter, Eleanor? We can't seem to find her," she said. Dada put a hand on her shoulder.

"Oh, hun," the teacher said apologetically. "Yes, I teach one of her classes. Eleanor wasn't . . ." the smiley teacher hesitated, looking down at me, Atticus, Monnie and Luna. "She wasn't feeling too well tonight, poor hun. She was looking forward to seeing y'all." The response sounded fake and automatic.

My heart seemed to sink to my toes, everything blurring, like when you try to hold back tears. I faintly remember Gran squeezing my shoulder with that wrinkled hand of hers, her maroon eyes glittering in the flashing lights. "I'm sorry, baby," she had whispered. "I'm here." The fact that Gran was being serious made things worse.

"You're still welcome to stay," the teacher added. "I'm Mrs. Plia, by the way." Mrs. Plia shook both my parents' hands, and they plastered on smiles though I saw the emotions scrolling through their eyes. Fear, worry, hurt, and anger were all there.

I saw Mrs. Plia whisper to Mama and Dada after she thought we weren't listening. I couldn't make out what she said, but her curiously teal eyes hidden behind those tiny glasses glittered.

Afterwards, my heart was hurting and I was fighting back tears. Monnie and Luna looked confused. "Where's Ellie, Momma?" whined Monnie. "I thought we were going to see Ellie!"

"She's sick, Monnie," Dada said thickly. "She can't come see us, not today." Luna's lower lip trembled, and Monnie's frown deepened. "Does anyone still want to stay at the party, though?" he asked. No one said anything. Even little Atticus was silent with the weight of everything. Around us, people were hugging, laughing, and one family, the mom, was happily crying.

"Let's hit the road."

The words Mama spoke then still echoed in my head. I took a deep breath and opened my eyes, pulling away from the flashback. Dada and Gran were staring at me warily.

A beat of silence passed, then the atmosphere relaxed.

"Bee, I've got to say! That was excellent control! I thought you were about to destroy your own house." Gran ran to me and enfolded me in a tight hug. "Just look at your Dada's shocked face. Tell me it isn't hilarious." She grinned, her face creasing even more.

I trilled a laugh that sounded like bells. It *was* kind of funny how his mouth hung open and his bright brown eyes popped out wide, but I was just glad that me and Gran were back to normal.

"If we could just avoid the topic of Eleanor right now, it might be easier," I said more quietly. "You know, to control . . ." I braced myself, thinking that they might get mad. I might have been slightly forgiving her, but I didn't want my dragon to take over, all the tingling . . . the voices . . . It made me shiver.

I was pretty sure Dada caught it, that small, timid, motion. His features melted just a little bit, softening. "Okay, Jellybean," he agreed. I searched his face, seeing the little green flecks in his sunny brown eyes, his laugh lines that slightly wrinkled his tanned face, his frizzed, thick, black beard. "Only for now, though. I raised you to face your problems, not run and hide from them."

"Okay," I answered, hating my voice for cracking. I waited as he shuffled over, joining our hug. His gruff, weathered hand stroked my back, making small circles. I felt Gran kiss my tangled hair, right then, a tiny sliver of hope gleamed inside me. *Maybe things will be okay after all*, I thought, the hope igniting deep in my heart.

Chapter 10. Eleanor, Not Ellie

That was when a knock rattled through the air.

Was it . . . I might have been having an asthma attack. *No, no, it couldn't be Eleanor.* Everyone was absolutely still as another knock shook in the air. This time, it sounded more unsure. But still, I knew that knock very, very well.

Knock, knock, knock. It was Eleanor's classic knocking, three firm but friendly short raps. I waited for Gran or Dada to answer the door, but instead Monnie skipped forward without a care in the world. I think my heart stopped for three whole beats. I saw Monnie's' face, almost in slow-mo, light up like the sun.

"Ellie!" Monnie squealed, jumping up and down, then round in circles. Finally, she collapsed into a hug.

"Hi, Monnie. I missed you." *Eleanor.* Her voice was kind of shy, but so smooth. It sounded like Grans' windchimes. And then she stepped through the door. I think my heart literally stopped.

Her hair fell in glossy black waves; she had obviously curled it. She also had gotten emerald highlights on her tips, a deep forest color green. I hated to say it, but they complimented her warm, bronze skin and shimmery gold eyes. I then realized: she wasn't wearing contacts! I felt heat rush over me. I was so happy I just said it.

"You- you're not wearing contacts." Ugh, I had stuttered! Color flooded my cheeks. A bright, cherry red color. "I mean, it looks good."

Eleanor gazed at me, but not for long. Her eyes flicked every which way, something she did when she was embarrassed. "Yeah, you know," she said. I didn't know, but I nodded while she shrugged. "Birming Dale likes to 'embrace your true self' or whatever. They were uncomfortable, anyway." She shrugged again. She was doing that a lot. We stared at each other for a long moment, until Dada butted in.

"Eleanor, my rosebud," he smiled warmly, but his bushy eyebrows settled high on his forehead with surprise. He hugged her. "We've missed you!" I sucked in a breath. "I didn't know you'd be here so soon. We would have ordered dinner already, maybe one of your favorites. Maria's pizzeria?"

"That's okay, Dada. I'm not too hungry," Eleanor replied. "And sorry for coming early, I just thought that with Blair's dragon and all, the quicker the better," she said, her voice quickening at the end. I froze. How did she know about me? Of course, I'd heard her voice. She'd told me she was coming, but I thought it was some weird dragon imagination thing. But if it wasn't, and she actually thought that, did that mean Hudson really said that, too?

I was worrying now. That meant Hudson knew that I could . . . that I was . . .

"A dragon?" Dada said, finishing my thoughts without even meaning to. "How did you know she Shifted already? Did Mama text?"

Gran stepped forward, sighing like she was bored. "No, you big hunk. Remember the spirit mind connection?" She rolled her brown-maroon eyes before focusing them on Eleanor. "Ellie, dearest! Welcome home." Gran too, embraced Eleanor.

"Gran," she said breathily, sinking into the hug. I didn't notice how tired she looked until now. It made me feel a little guilty about our awkward encounter. Maybe I should have hugged her. That would have cleared up some of that awkward gunk; we were never weird with each other like that before. I sighed heavily. I was tired too.

"Mama will be disappointed she didn't get to greet you right away," Dada mused, trying like usual to gruffly make a joke that wasn't funny. I saw it only made Eleanor shyer, throwing looks around the room.

She was like this around strangers, but never us. Were we the same thing now?

"I'm kidding, Ellie," he huffed. "I mean, Eleanor." Finally, this made Eleanor laugh.

"It's okay, I'm over that stupid phase," Eleanor promised, lightly laughing and slightly rolling her glittery gold eyes. "Eleanor is so formal."

"Oh, good," Dada huffed. "Blair will have to tell you how many times I slipped up with that." He was nudging me to talk with Eleanor, obviously. The fact that he was trying was sweet enough that Eleanor looked over at me and smiled in a way only sisters will understand. I gazed back, my lips twitching, but not totally smiling. I wasn't quite ready for that, though I wanted to be.

Dada grinned, proud of our sisterly exchange. I had to admit, I felt a little like grinning too. Gran slid in between me and Eleanor, smugly smiling. She placed a withered hand on both our shoulders. "Let it out, girls, let it out," she said. We both couldn't help it.

We smiled.

After that, Eleanor dove into all about her school and what it was like, who was nice and who wasn't. Stuff like that.

She definitely was opening up. I felt good just to hear her voice again, smooth and clear. It seemed to cheer up our whole house, the couches fluffing themselves and the towers straightening.

Eleanor told us Birming Dale was massive and confusing. She said she's gotten lost about millions of times, even in the cafeteria. But she loved it there, she told us. "It's a lot like here," she said. "Tall rather than wide, with big limestone bricks that hold up the spinning towers. Bad landscaping, too."

Dada chuckled at that, but I bit my lip. Didn't she know we'd seen her school before, on visiting day? Yeah, that day, the one where she was 'sick'. It made me think of Mrs. Plia, that jolly teacher who'd called us hun.

"Do you know Mrs. Plia?" I asked her.

Eleanor smiled in response, her eyes far away as she said, "Oh, yeah, she's nice. Super peppy and jolly." Then she realized. "Wait, how do you know her?"

I shrugged, mimicking her from before. I avoided her eyes. "Visiting day."

"Oh," Eleanor swallowed. "I was going to wait until Mama got back, but now that you've brought it up . . ." She sighed. "I'm sorry. I wasn't really sick, I just missed you guys so much and if I saw you, I worried it would bring up my dragon and . . . Look, I'm so sorry. I was confused back then. Now I know you can't just avoid who you love because you're afraid of something that's a part of you. I know that now." She scanned at all the faces in the room, stopping on me. "Blair, you get it, right?"

I didn't answer. I was locked on something else she'd said. "You have a dragon?" I whispered. I had assumed it anyway, but now that it was confirmed . . . I looked at her fiercely.

"Wait, you didn't tell her?" asked Eleanor, sounding slightly enraged. She searched Dada's face. "Why not?" she demanded.

Dada looked down. He mumbled something that sounded like, "no time."

"Well." Eleanor inhaled deeply and dusted her hands off, though she had nothing on them. Then, she spun on her heels to turn and face me, her stare unsettling. It made me itch.

"I guess I'll explain, then," she began, and I listened with all my heart.

"So, you know the legends. Guess what? They're all true!" shouted Eleanor, making me jump at her volume. "The wind gods gave us this magical power stone, but then Luna, who had beef with the leader god, gave it to the sea people. That made the wind gods super angry, and they were like, 'Girl! Luna, why'd you do that?' so they sought it back. But when they did, its power had faded some, so now a select few people can Shift into dragons. Ta-da." Her voice was rushed and kind of bitter. "You ever wonder why we have gold eyes, Blair? Here's your answer, on a silver platter."

Dada huffed slightly. "That's not the way I would put it, but true enough. And the gold eyes are just an odd genetic manipulation that only occurs to Wind Shifters."

"Wind Shifters?" I wondered. "So, there are other kinds?"

"Fire Shifters," Dada hissed harshly, his tone loaded with venom. "Nasty people, Blair. Stay away from them whenever you can. They sent spies into our villages! They stole our secret on how to Shift," continued Dada, his voice rising. "Of course," his tone was smug now, "very few could manage dragon-Shifting. And for them, the eye color is teal." He shrugged. "I don't know why, it just is. And let me just say, gold is way cooler."

I forced a laugh. Things sort of made sense. I wanted to ask how this actually happened; like, come on, did I really believe in magical, powerful gemstones and shape-Shifting? But I knew it wasn't the right thing to say. I just nodded instead.

"Yes, mm-hmm," said Eleanor thoughtfully. "What else . . . Oh! When you're new to Shifting, your dragon is triggered by stress, panic, anger." For everything she said, she ticked off one of her fingers. "You know, something you're worrying about."

I looked intently at my feet. Eleanor was the reason that triggered my first Shift.

"Wow, look who's suddenly an expert," Gran teased, making the color rush to Eleanor's cheeks.

"School has been helping," she said bashfully, and I was so preoccupied watching her tuck a strand of hair behind her ear that it took me a second to grasp what he was saying.

"Your school?" I gaped, scanning her face. "Birming Dale High? It's a school of arts," I continued, though by her frown it seemed like more.

"Oh my spirits, you really didn't tell her anything!" Eleanor cried. Dada raised an eyebrow at her sass but said nothing. "Well, okay, here's the secret; Birming Dale is really about teaching Shifting and dragons and legends."

Wow, I guess my Harry Potter guesses weren't too far off after all.

"You can start there too, I think. Next semester," she added, smiling in a shiny way. "They have this program for under-age Shifters you'll love. It's so much better than real school! Plus, they have an awesome legends elective . . ."

Her voice faded as I drowned in all these new thoughts. I said nothing. I couldn't even picture it: me, learning to be a dragon? "So, you like it there?" was all I said.

"Well, yeah," replied Eleanor awkwardly. "You will too!"

"I don't know," I said angrily. She was just having the greatest time without us, now wasn't she? And here she was, rubbing it in. "But I do know I won't have anywhere near the amount of fun you're having. Because I actually care about this family!" I yelled.

Eleanor looked stricken for half a second, then anger clouded her face. "You have no idea how much I care," she said, sounding dark.

I shook my head twice and hard, whirling my dark hair around my head; a tornado. "I'm not blind, Eleanor. I'm not stupid." Tears welled in my eyes before I sprinted to my room, before I could see the cross look on Dada's face.

Of course, it wasn't all my room. I shared it . . . with Eleanor.

I shuddered. Why did she even bother coming here if she was just going to lie about everything? If she really cared, she wouldn't have left. If she really, truly cared, she wouldn't have ghosted us. We were like a masterpiece ripped down the middle. And if she wasn't going to patch us back up, we might as well start over.

I grimaced as that tingling erupted inside me. The little ants, crawling just beneath my skin. I shook away the feelings and calmed before I could get to the voices.

Ugh, the voices. They were the worst part.

I had my eyes closed, but I heard the door creak open and someone come in. I whipped my head up, and it was . . . Mama? She must have gotten home from work. I looked up at her, tears streaming down my face.

"Oh, baby," Mama soothed. I sobbed harder, so hard I could barely seem to breathe. Mama just sat there, her arm around me until I calmed down. When I did, she looked at me, her face scrolling emotions a mile a minute. Shock, worry, love.

"I know a lot is going on right now." She sighed, the heavy, weighted, sound sinking into the air. Yet a second later, a smile propped up on her face. Her brown eyes lit; a campfire amidst the dark. "But you're my strong girl, Bee-Bee. I know you can handle things." She pointedly stared at me. "The *right* way."

I felt my stomach churn. So she knew the gist. The way she was looking at me did seem to give me strength, though. Her gaze was warm and powerful although it was expectant.

"I know you can do that," Mama said softly.

"I can," I whispered confidently, because right now, all I wanted to do was please Mama. Her brown eyes shone. She smiled tiredly, her face the picture of sadness and remembrance.

"You and Ellie were so close before." She sighed. "I hate how there's a before and after now. Literally, it's been a month!" She looked up at me. "Man, you can hold a grudge, Blair."

Finally I laughed. It felt good.

Mama smiled, and my heart glowed so bright it shined a spotlight right through my body. Then she smiled and slowly got up, her hand on my shoulder. "We're going out to eat for dinner, so get ready." I wanted to complain, but didn't. Mama grinned, squeezing my shoulder.

"Love you, Blair," she said.

"Love you too," I whispered.

Mama headed out, and I flopped back onto my bed. *This was going to be hard*, I sighed. *A family dinner?* Then I whipped my head up. I was making this a million times harder. She's just Eleanor! I was going to try. I was going to be strong, like Mama said.

I brushed my hair, but there wasn't much I could do with the frizzy mess. I changed, because I wanted to feel fresh, into a fancier than needed dress. It had a cinched top, and was dotted with yellow flowers. I smiled very slightly, thinking it would go nicely with my sandals.

I came out of my bedroom. I saw Eleanor giving Mama the run through she'd given us.

"There's this girl, Shyla, in my Shifting class. She's amazing," Eleanor smiled. "We're becoming friends, I think," Eleanor smiled. She looked so happy.

"That's great, sweetheart!" Mama grinned. "Any teachers who're nice?"

Eleanor nodded, looking hyper. "Yeah, the professor who teaches my Shifting class is also nice. Mrs. Plia? Blair told me you met her."

"Right, right," Mama said thoughtfully. I had a feeling, that like me, she didn't quite want to relieve those moments yet. "She was nice."

"Now, Ellie," Dada changed the subject, "this is the most important. Are there any particular boys-"

"Dada!" Eleanor squealed.

"He's got a valid point, my dear." Gran grinned, and I could practically feel the spirits in the room lifting.

"Well, I don't like anyone," Eleanor sniffed. I giggled and sat down on the couch. I could feel Mama smile. Eleanor, who was holding Atticus, groaned. Luna and Monnie joined in on my snickers.

"Not you guys, too!" she cried, burying her face into Atticus's chubby baby body. My lips twitched as Atticus let out a high laugh, mischievously pulling on Eleanor's big hoop earrings.

She yelped. "Naughty Atticus," she reprimanded. Everyone laughed.

"Guys, I'm hungry." Monnie announced. In the background, Luna chorused a 'me too'. In addition, someone's stomach grumbled. It might have been Eleanor's.

"Well, I think that does it," Gran huffed. "What are we waiting for?"

Chapter 11. Dinner

I stirred my soup hypnotically. Like Eleanor had said, I wasn't that hungry. Besides, when you stir your soup as much as I was stirring, it gets cold. I stirred round and round so it made a little whirlpool. Then I stirred the other way. The creamy, red tomato flavor and bright green spinach normally would have been delicious, but my stomach quivered in protest.

That's when I felt the tap on my shoulder.

I looked up. "Huh?"

Eleanor looked eager, reminding me of a two-year-old thinking of stealing a cookie. Her gold eyes glinted, as she rapidly brushed invisible tangles out of her chocolate hair. I found myself staring at those green tips. I hated them so much that I loved them.

"Look, the new neighbors," she hissed, mouth twitching like it always did every time she gossiped. "Dada said they moved from Maine. Isn't that far? And I thought Birming Dale was a hike!" She rolled her eyes. I knew she was begging me to talk, to gossip like teen sisters normally did.

For one, we both weren't quite normal.

And two, I was frozen looking at the boy in front of me. He walked casually to the table two down from us, and I leaned on the back two legs of my chair to take him in. Perfect blonde ringlets that circled his head like a crown. Rosy cheeks and a smirk for a smile. Yes, I knew this boy.

Hudson.

My heart burned, and I couldn't tell if it was in a good way or not.

"Blair, are you good?" asked Eleanor, shaking my shoulder again. "Seriously, nowadays I have no idea what's going on in your head."

"Right back at you," I chuckled.

"So then, you'll have to tell me," she retorted. I raised an eyebrow, knowing she had something up her sleeve. "What's with blondie?" Her full lips twitched. I began to play dumb. "Oh, save it, Blair. I'm your older sister and anyway, I can see the way you looked at him."

My cheeks set aflame. "I don't," I said harshly, sneaking another peak at Hudson, who was sitting across from who I thought to be his mom. "And, anyway," I sniffed, "his hair is more golden, not blonde. Blondes are not my type."

"So he is your type, then! You admit it," shrieked Eleanor.

"What?" I said, stirring my soup faster. "Can we drop this, please?" I sighed. Eleanor shrugged, glancing sideways at Hudson. She looked thoughtful.

"What's his name?"

I shot her a look. "Seriously-"

"What's his name?" Eleanor asked again, patiently.

"Hudson," I grumbled. I shifted my weight and finally took a spoonful of soup. That's when Hudson saw me. His teal eyes lingered on me for a few seconds, then drifted back to his food. They reminded me of the sea, lapping forward and lapping back. I watched as he shook his curls away from his face, and I anticipated. Was he going to ignore me or . . .?

I got my answer within a span of seconds. Calmly, Hudson said something to his mom and casually walked over. His features were as smooth as pearls, his eyes glittering like sapphires. Inwardly, I wondered how he had the courage to walk up to us at all.

"Hi, Blair." He smiled tentatively.

My breath caught. "Hi," I said cautiously. His pink lips twitched slightly, and I thought he might be holding back a smirk. This made me snicker, and I realized my whole family was staring expectantly.

Hudson shook his curls and they bounced delightfully. It seemed to be a habit he had, one that happened to be very soothing to watch. He looked at my parents. "Mr. and Mrs. Norwillo, right?" Mama and Dadas' faces collapsed into warm smiles. I knew they liked it when people called them using their last names.

"Yes, that's us," Mama said, the twinkly sound of contempt filling her voice. I started to relax into Hudson's' charm. Things were going fine.

"We met today by the creek. It's a nice place. You guys are lucky to live here," he smiled sweetly. "I moved from Maine, actually, and it's freezing there."

"I bet," Dada said, his deep voice sounding slightly cautious. I knew he wasn't loving the fact that this boy was what had kept me up at the creek that day, when I was gone for hours . . . Thinking of the creek made me remember Shifting, and how I saw someone watching me. My breath quickened, but Hudson was oblivious; chatting aimlessly with Mama and Dada and Gran. Instantly, it reminded me that I needed to talk to him about it. What if he told someone about seeing a fifteen-foot gold dragon? Plus, I didn't know how long he was watching me for. Did he even know it was me, or was I safe? And by safe, I meant that I had jeopardized the dragon population.

My thoughts churned, an unruly ocean. Each wave brought a worry; Hudson, Shifting, dragons, Eleanor. Eventually, the waves would merge together and crash down . . . I cringed. That was a dark analogy.

I was just about to join in on the conversation when I noticed

Hudson's' mom walking up. She wore a professional looking blazer, and her hair was pulled back so tightly it looked painful. It was average brown colored with silver strands tucked in, and very straight. Not at all like Hudson with his flowy, natural curls and golden blonde hair. She had a pinched face and tiny wrinkles etched across her pasty, pale skin. Her lips were set into a line. The only thing she seemed to share with Hudson was the teal eyes, glittering like the Caribbean Sea.

Otherwise, Hudson's' mom looked the complete opposite of him. Uninviting, scary and a little principal-like. I imagined tiny glasses on her and cringed.

She walked over closer, her black heels clacking against the pavement. The sound made my heart race for no reason. "Hello," she announced. Her voice did not seem to match her icy eyes and pained face; it was jolly and had a slight British accent. "I'm Imogen. Hudson's' mother." She smiled tightly. Her eyes glinted as she grabbed Hudson's shoulder and squeezed it. To some it may have seemed motherly, but it looked painful as she dug her nails into him. I caught Hudson straightening up, like he was a stretched rubber band right before it snapped.

With horror, I stared at her. Something was up about her, and though I didn't know what, I knew for sure one thing.

I did not like Imogen Ignis.

Not at all.

After about five minutes, I sighed. "I'm going to go to the bathroom." I was starting to get sick of Imogen's peppy voice and icy glares.

"I'll come." It was Hudson. He glanced at me cautiously and also his mom. Her lips twitched in reply, but she nodded primly.

I speed walked away, Hudson trailing behind me coolly, hands in his jean pockets. "You're dressed up," he stated. I whipped around a shot with a withering look. Didn't he know it was a deathly offense to comment on a girl's outfit?

"Well, I've never seen a thirteen-year-old boy wear jeans before," I replied, throwing a pathetic look behind my shoulder.

He cocked an eyebrow. "Really? Weird."

"Especially not in this weather," I continued. "It's hot here. Deal with it," I snorted, flicking my dark hair. Inwardly, I felt a teensy bit proud. *Comebacks,* I thought smugly. *Comebacks.*

"Still," he replied. I had a feeling my cheeks were on literal fire as he observed me. "It looks nice - I didn't say it didn't! Chill." Of course. He always had a way to turn things around. I didn't want to admit it, but my insides were glowing.

"Thanks," I mumbled. We'd reached the bathroom and were standing awkwardly. This was my chance. "Hudson." I tried to keep my voice even. "Did you visit the creek after we met?" I asked. How to phrase things was difficult.

"Oh yeah," Hudson replied. "Serious, Blair, that place is awesome."

I grinned. "Right?" It was fun that we both shared something. It was also fun because Hudson deemed no memory over what had happened. Must have been an animal, I presumed. Maybe it was an owl or something.

I breathed a sigh of relief. It felt like a weight had been lifted off my shoulders. "Okay. Got to go," I said, ducking into the ladies' restroom. The last thing I saw was Hudson's' impish grin.

The bathroom here was an average bathroom. Blue tiled floors, a small sink and the foamy soap dispenser. I'd been here many times, but this time, it seemed everything was closing in. That tingly feeling overcame me quickly and I rushed out before I could Shift.

Hudson was waiting, leaning against the wall. His fingers tapped and slapped the wall, creating a steady beat. I watched for a few moments, waiting for the urge to Shift disperse. Hudson looked up suddenly, looking surprised. Then he noticed my expression and frowned. "You good?" he asked.

"Fine," I said, trying to laugh off my bright red cheeks. My heart sank. Was this what it was going to be like every day of my life, from now on? Trying to keep my emotions in check, to not Shift. To lie to everyone who didn't know about . . . Being a dragon? I pressed my lips tightly together.

Dada and Mama had told me there was going to be a ritual tonight. At first, I thought they were joking. A ritual? But their hard looks and creased foreheads said otherwise. The caterpillars, forgotten in my stomach, emerged into total butterflies. What would it be like?

Hudson and I walked in silence. I was so worried I almost didn't notice his face; far away in his thoughts. "You okay?" I repeated what he'd asked me earlier.

"Yeah, I just . . ." His pale cheeks exploded with color, looking kind of cute. I tried to focus. "A lot of things are difficult. You know, it'll figure itself out. Things will get easier, I promise. I know! Sure, it's different, and strange, and . . . well," he sighed. I didn't know who he was talking to, himself or me. It kind of felt like he was describing . . . Shifting. Of course, he had to prove me wrong. "Moving, I mean. It's just a lot," he added.

I nodded politely as we stepped back to our families. His mom had drifted off back to her table, now scrolling on her phone. Everyone chatted warmly at ours, except Gran, who stared at Imogen. I shivered.

"You know," Hudson added. "We should meet up sometime. You

could show me around," he said, grinning.

    My heart jumped. I found myself saying okay and if we wanted to meet up tomorrow, on Thursday. I also found him saying yes. Longingly, he glanced toward where my family was sitting, then wheeled away to his mom. I turned to walk to my family too, and I couldn't help but smile.

Chapter 10. My Ritual

I stared at the flickering fire. It shed a soft, warm glow across people's faces, giving the whole place an ominous feel. Though people talked, it was in feathery whispers and too complex to understand.

I itched at my top. It was a cultural tradition for girls to wear leathery clothes, a long skirt and sleeveless top, decorated with dried plants and clay beads. Let's just say it wasn't comfortable.

I kept thinking, this is it? This is the ritual?

I looked at my parents. I stood close to them for comfort. They were having an intense conversation with a girl with really short brown hair and a very freckled face. I didn't bother to listen. Right when I was both nervous and bored out of my mind, a short stubby old man clapped his hands.

"Attention! In a few short moments, the ritual will begin!"

There were a few claps, some nods of approval and one whistle. All I wanted to do was puke.

We took our seats on the dirty ground, wishing for once our community would take better care of landscaping. Eleanor was there too, looking like a ghost, and so was Gran. Except she got a fancy chair in the center of everything. I wasn't sure why.

The old man added some more wood to the fire, and it sprung up hungrily. Smoke swirled in the air, filling my nostrils with the scent. Eleanor leaned toward me, her hand cupped over her mouth.

"They're about to talk in this gibberish no one understands," she explained. I nodded eagerly; at least she was giving me information! "Then they tell some legends. You know, the one about the power stone. And then," her voice dropped lower, "you have to Shift, Blair. You walk up there and Shift." Her expression was serious, but I couldn't help not believing her.

"Oh, come on," I scoffed. Then I started to worry; she was serious! "What if I forget how? An-and in front of everyone!?"

Eleanor glanced away, showing a hint of a smile. "I think you can do it," she said softly. I felt my heart swell with her words. And then she cleared her throat. "Anyway, after that, they give you the gist; we're wind dragons, there are also fire dragons, they're evil, by the way. You can only be a wind dragon if you have gold eyes. The voices you hear before you Shift are other spirits, guiding you. You also have an opportunity to come to Birming Dale next semester," she offered. "And-"

"Wait, slow down," I blinked. "There are other types of dragons? And this gold eyes thing . . . does that mean they knew I'd be a dragon all along? And you too?" I gasped. "Why didn't they warn us, then?" I demanded.

Eleanor just shook her head. "It was for the better, Blair." Then she laughed, "Ha! I sound like mom and dad."

I grimaced. "But why-" It felt like my head had exploded with questions. Of course, I was cut off by the squeal of a microphone too close to someone's mouth; high-pitched and ear splitting.

"Sorry, folks," a voice said. It took a second for me to realize it came from the old man. He was now sitting next to Gran on those big, formal chairs. I caught Gran's gaze and could have sworn she winked. Then the old man's voice blasted through the hot air once again.

"Let us begin," he said, and I took a deep breath to steady my nerves.

The old, short man with the long white beard smiled warmly and introduced himself with a long name I could never pronounce. He had a gentle, soothing voice that caressed over my nerves, unraveling them slightly, but they didn't disappear completely.

"This time is a very special chapter in a child's life. The first Shift will represent courage, cleverness and greatest of all, the transition into adulthood." I shivered, and people around me clapped politely. The old man continued.

"We happily welcome another great Shifter to protect us. Being a Shifter is a crucial role in our community, as you can probably understand. Despite your young age, Blair Norwillo," he said, and I worried, I was young? "You are expected to be as responsible as any other Shifter. I'm sure your family can ease this transition greatly, especially your eldest sister."

He smiled. I just nodded along, staring him in the eyes pretending I didn't have a million questions buzzing around. How the heck did he know everything about me? And why was he talking about my family in front of —I glanced around— maybe fifty strangers.

"Next to me," he continued, "   is Victoria Norwillo, who ironically happens to be the grandmother of the blooming Shifter we are celebrating tonight." An excited whoop echoed into the air, and there were some more whistles. Why was Gran famous?

Gran stepped out of her fancy chair, waving elegantly like a celebrity, or no, a queen. "Welcome," she said gracefully. I watched, mesmerized. I always thought that Gran was really in her twenties but disguised as an old woman, yet this only seemed to prove me more right. "How exciting we are celebrating another Shift, so soon! It's great to see you all."

Her maroon eyes flickered in the firelight, her silver hair dancing. "I've been doing this for a while," she said, and people chuckled along. "As you know, I am your Teller," she announced, making me frown.

"Teller?" I whispered to Eleanor. "I don't get what's happening . . . Gran's famous. This old guy is talking to me in front of everyone like, I don't know, a weirdo? He knows about me, you, all of us!" I was out of breath.

"Yeah, it's overwhelming, I know," Eleanor shrugged. "Okay, so, let me explain." I nodded eagerly. "Gran is actually this super cool fortune teller lady, and she can see glimpses of the future. It's shaky, because most things aren't totally decided until the second before, but still. Cool." She shrugged. I think my eyebrows may have popped off my forehead.

"You know when Gran has those bad days, where she doesn't feel well or has a headache? Well, that actually means she's looking into the future, finding ways to help our community strengthen.

"And, she can also give out prophecies. It's very rare, but it's happened a few times – I learned about it in history!" Eleanor beamed, clearly happy to snatch up that big sister, know-it-all role.

"Okay," I said shakily. "But how does he know about me? I've never seen him in my life, and he's announcing my life to more strangers and . . ." I held back a sob, my insides bubbling up higher.

"Hey, it's okay," Eleanor said, her voice smoothing over at the edges. "Look, I know it's crazy, but," she paused as she collected her thoughts. "But hey, look at me! I went through this just like you."

Sheepishly, I glanced at her. She did look glamorous; her dark hair weaved into many tiny braids, the leather top with the clay beads fit around her perfectly. If she got through this, and was still perfectly beautiful, then maybe I could too. That's when I remembered something.

"Well, you are older than me," I mumbled. "I didn't realize that." My mood dipped again, and I threw up my hands. "See, even that old dude knows more about me than I do!"

Eleanor stared hard into me, her gold eyes intense. "Blair, come on. I know it's a lot. I get it, but you have to just-"

"Just what, Eleanor?" I snapped, interrupting her as my voice climbed higher.

"Go with the flow," she said bitterly, sending multiple glances our way.

I scoffed and rolled my eyes. "Oh, okay, thanks, I'll make sure to *go with the flow*," I said, sarcasm slithering into my voice. "And the old dude said you'd be helpful! Finally, I know something more than him," I remarked.

Eleanor glared. "Well, at least I'm not narcissistic. And I know you better shut up if you don't want to get kicked out of here." Her words hit me hard in the chest, a blow that left me pondering.

"What?" I hissed, but Eleanor ignored me. I then tried to tune into what the old guy was saying, but only gibberish came out. It was the language of the wind people.

I thought about what Eleanor had said. Narcissistic? What did she mean by that? It wasn't like I stared at myself for hours every day thinking I was so pretty!

Longingly, I stared up at the stars as if they were to guide me. Instead they sneered at me, teasing me with their sheer beauty. I glared at the glistening, evil fire balls, and tried to focus on what the old man was saying. Gibberish flew from his mouth, fast as a stream. He was speaking the Wind Language.

As I listened to the smooth, elegant words that slipped out of his mouth, the words I didn't understand, I started to slowly become more relaxed. I imagined his words as the breeze, shuffling the leaves on trees and ruffling the spurts of grass persistently protruding from the ground. Sometimes the wind picked up with a howl, occasionally when the old announcer got especially passionate.

Suddenly, the wind halted and everything was still and quiet. Almost too still and quiet. Awkwardly, I opened my eyes, which I hadn't even realized were closed. Instantly, I noticed two things.

One, it was darker than it should have been.

And two, everyone was staring expectantly. At me.

Chapter 11. The Voice

"Sorry, what?" I mumbled, trying not to offend anyone. I knew my cheeks were on fire; I could feel them burning through my flesh.

"Time to Shift, my dear," the old man said, and his voice contained two sides; a gentle one, and a slightly more important, let's-get-this-over-with one.

I tried to not focus on the second voice.

"Okay," was all I said, or rather whispered. So many people were staring. Each pair of eyes snapped at me with cruel eagerness. Although the stares probably weren't the worst of my problems . . . How do you Shift, again? I wondered frantically. My first Shift and my only Shift, was accidental. How were you supposed to replicate that? I had just got so freaked out, and upset . . .

When you're new to Shifting, your dragon is triggered by stress, panic, anger. That's what Eleanor had told me, at least. So I had to think of what scared me, made me angry . . .

And that was Eleanor.

I took a deep breath and began. I imagined my power a lit match, and I had to add the kindling. My thoughts swirled with heat, and that's when I felt the tingling. I wanted to stop Shifting immediately. But I didn't. I had to do this.

This time the tingle was worse, more like a searing burn. It scorched my insides, and my heart seemed to scrape against my ribs to get away from the heat. Suddenly, though, everything soothed as one single voice echoed in my head. A voice that sent shivers down my spine.

Soon, child, you, your family and your whole House will be sucked into my trap, it cooed. The voice sounded nice and happy, except the words coming from it were cruel and terrifying. But that voice; it sounded so familiar! I racked my brain, but the answer lingered on the tip of my tongue. Again, I shivered. I could think about that later; right now, more voices were starting to pelt me. At least they were nice ones.

Come on, sweetie!
Ooh, good luck.
Happy ritual!
You got this.

None of the voices I knew, which I couldn't decide if that was nice or awkward. I just couldn't place that one other voice . . . it felt a million miles away, but also less than an inch. Ugh!

Finally it ended. With relief, I snuffled in a breath using my whole dragon body. Everything was now sharpened into focus, like when a person who can't see that well first gets glasses. People leaned back when I let out a proud howl, although some smiled and clapped. But soon everyone erupted with cheers. I saw that girl Mama and Dada were talking to earlier, with the splotchy freckles dotting her face.

It also smelled amazing, out here in the deep woods. I imagined that the forest here smelled as good to dragon-me as a cake did to normal-me. The grass was fresh and tangy, and the leaves sent the smells of earthy dirt and freshwater straight to me.

Gran smiled proudly at me and so did the old man. "Well done, very nice." I lifted my head with pride, spotting Eleanor with the motion. She stared at me with wonder and ice in her eyes. I imagined how I looked to all them; looming tall, my gold scales flickering mysteriously in the firelight. Of course it felt weird, for strangers to be staring at me open-mouthed, clapping. It felt like they knew a secret about me I didn't know myself, and they all were humoring me.

Still, it felt amazing. My glimmering wings flapped gracefully, and for the first time in my life, I felt powerful. And for all these people to see me in my best state, well, it felt good.

Soon the old man announced for me to turn back. Half reluctant, half relieved, I obeyed. Dada was right - the first time was the worst. This time after Shifting, I was grinning crazily and not sobbing.

And that wrapped it up. The ritual was over with, and I felt happy. Like I was floating above everyone. People congratulated me and clapped me on the back, and I smiled back to the strangers. As we walked out, Gran's voice blared through a microphone. Respectfully everyone stopped and listened. When I heard her voice cold and cautious, my stomach sank. What was going on?

"Before we depart," she said, her tone important but volume soft. "We need to share some information." Peoples' murmurs started to fly, hushed whispers and mumbles that zipped from ear to ear.

"As you know, our sworn enemy House is the Fire Nation. They stole our secret on how to Shift and stormed our villages . . ." Her face grew angrier and her wrinkled bronze skin shifted into reds as she went on. "And, although we have predicted this for years, it has been confirmed. We are at war with each other."

Confusion burst inside me. If we were at war, what did that mean? Were we going to battle each other? Someone shouted out a better question:

"Why now, if it's been thought about for years?" The voice might have belonged to the freckled face girl with short brown hair, but I couldn't be sure.

"A reasonable question," the old man said, glancing at Gran. "One we're not quite sure of the answer to currently."

People made outraged cries, blurs of confusion, anger, and worry. The old man fought to explain further over the swell of anxious voices. "Vic, right here," he gestured to Gran, "as you know is our Teller. Over the past months she has tried to see what our enemies have been up to, but their decision was undecided - until now. For an undetermined reason, they decided to signal war." He sighed. "I'm very sorry. We will get back to you as soon as we know more."

My stomach churned with nerves. War. Anxiously I glanced toward my family. Dada looked broken, and Mama looked extremely worried. And Eleanor . . . well, I couldn't look at her.

We were the last ones to leave. Mobs of people swarmed around Gran and the old man, questioning them. Finally Gran and the old man wearily walked toward us, unsmiling. "That was a lot," Gran said, grabbing hold of my hand and Eleanor's.

"Are we really going to war, Gran?" Eleanor said softly.

"I'm afraid so, Ellie dear," she said, maroon eyes flickering. "About that, Manny and I have to tell you something."

I couldn't help it, I laughed. "Manny?" I asked, then swallowed, hoping I wasn't being offensive. The old man, or Manny, was walking right with us. "Sorry," I said, cheeks flushed.

Manny laughed along, and so did Gran. Soon everyone joined in. "Yes, I know it's funny," he chuckled. "I've heard a lot about my name over the years. My true name is Emmanuel. But your grandmother here started to call me Manny, and let's just say it stuck."

"Just like you call me Vic," she bantered. "I needed a nickname for you too!"

"Okay, what were you going to tell us?" Mama said tiredly, interrupting their playful conversation. I couldn't be sure in the darkness, but they both might have been blushing.

"Well," Manny said, clearing his throat, "we didn't tell the others this because we suspected they would become more uneasy," he sighed. "But you must know, Norwillo family. Especially you, Eleanor and Blair. The Fire Nation is coming. Vic predicts they'll be here by July first."

I saw Dada check his watch. "That's only seven days away," he said shakily. I don't think that's enough time."

"Nor do I," Gran said gravely. "But we cannot thwart their attempts. They have strengthened over the years, and it seems they have somehow gained inside information."

"A spy," Manny hissed. "Rotten people, the Fire Nation." Deeply, he inhaled as if to calm himself.

"What about . . ." Eleanor started, thoughtfully gazing into the endless void. "No, never mind." She shrugged. "I had a suspicion for who the spy was, but," she shook her head, "no way."

"Ellie, we're open to all suggestions right now," Mama said, sounding strained. "Any idea is valued."

"Okay, okay, well," Eleanor said, her glossy hair shining in the full moon, her eyes seeming to flick everywhere, weighing options. "I was thinking about that boy and his mother. The . . . what's their name? Oh, the Ignis'. Hudson and the mom-"

"Imogen," Manny finished, nodding. "Welcomed them into the community yesterday. Nice boy, but the mom . . . seemed a little strange. Moved from Maine, correct?" he said, his voice far away. He twirled his thin white hair, blanketed in deep thoughts.

"Actually, this could make sense," Mama said excitedly. A bad feeling, a feeling of dread, jumped inside me. Hudson would never, right? After all things our Wind Nation said about the 'horrible' Fire Nation, Hudson didn't seem to match the description. Imogen, on the other hand, maybe. "Hudson had teal eyes, remember? So did his mom. That could mean they were Fire Shifters," she said.

"And the blonde hair," Dada said disdainfully. "I should've known." He turned to me. "Blair, you met him first. He walked you to the bathroom, for spirits' sake! Did he say anything, give any hints?"

"I don't know," I muttered, replaying all my moments with him in my head. "But sometimes it felt like he knew stuff about me," I said very quietly.

"Like what?" Gran pressed.

"I don't know," I repeated. "I was probably hallucinating, but I think I saw a pair of teal eyes watching me once I was a dragon." Everyone gasped. "I don't know if he saw me Shift, or just saw dragon-me, or if I was going insane. But whoever those teal eyes belonged to, they weren't scared of me. They just . . . watched."

Dada pulled me closer into him, his voice gruff as he asked, "Anything else?"

Carefully I picked out my words. I didn't want to say that I'd heard his voice when I first Shifted; that seemed too big and scary. Instead I said, "Well, he said something about even though things were probably weird and difficult right now, they'd work themselves out? I don't really remember. But it felt like he knew I Shifted."

Gran shook her head frantically. "Oh my spirits, this is bad. If all this is true, and they really do know, we're doomed." Her creased face wobbled with worry, the lines etching deeper into her tanned skin.

Manny shook his head slowly. "Let's sleep on it, alright?" he suggested, and I noticed his lavender eyelids.

"No, no, don't we need a plan?" Dada cut in. "Tomorrow there'll be only six days until the battle. What can we do to help?"

"More importantly," Mama added, grabbing Dada's hand, "why are we fighting anyway? I know they're our enemies, but . . ."

"Power," Gran and Manny said in perfect unison. Gran continued and Manny smiled. "That's what most humans want these days; money and power. If they could control us, since they're already allied with Earth Nation and Water Nation is neutral, then they would gain Full Elemental Power."

"What's that-"

"Bad," Gran said. "Extremely bad. Us, the Wind Nation, would lose the ability to Shift," she paused for effect, "and while we lose our power, their power would amplify twenty times greater than it was before." She looked at us, a deep, ancient, worry in her eyes. "They'd be absolutely unbeatable. We must not let that happen."

I felt it in the air right then. The steely determination, the powerful courage.

"We're going to win this war," I said confidently.

"Yes," Manny agreed. "And you know why? Because you're going to be our Wind Nation Guardian, protector of the power source."

Chapter 12. The Prophecy

"But seriously? Guardian? That's the most basic name in history," I complained. Honestly, the title Guardian was cool; I just thought maybe if I made a joke it would lighten the mood.

It didn't.

"Sure, it might be boring, but it's straightforward," insisted Manny, not getting that I was joking. "You're young, and younglings are always the most powerful Shifters. Plus, you come from a powerful family." He glanced around, his gaze lingering on Gran.

"But I don't know how to control it yet!" I protested. "What if I mess up? There has to be a more experienced, better Shifter," I pleaded. "Even Eleanor."

"You showed some excellent control tonight," Gran said supportively. "You'll be a great Guardian." My brow furrowed. There was something going on here that they weren't saying. I only Shifted yesterday and had no training . . .

"There's something weird about that reasoning," Eleanor edged, suspicious.

It only lasted a millisecond. Gran and Manny shared a look; a deep, thoughtful, what-do-we-do look. Quickly they became themselves again, and Manny spoke up. "You're right," he said shamefully. "You've been chosen because of the Prophecy."

"What Prophecy!?" we all exclaimed.

"Shh, you'll wake the birds." Gran dodged the question with calmness and ease.

"Gran, *what Prophecy*!?" I hissed. If everything really was going to depend on me, I had to know what was going on. Eleanor shot me a look that said, *relax*. I glared right back, a glare that protested, *just a second ago you were screaming too!*

Manny sighed deeply. "I'm so very sorry. It's just, we're the older ones here, and that urges us to protect you from all the nail-biting, crazy, angering, information. You understand, don't you?"

"Look, Manny," Eleanor said gently and firmly, "we want to help. Actually, we'll need to help if we're going to win this war. So you're going to have to trust us a bit more. Give us reports, and we'll also report to you. We can do this. I know we can! But only if . . . we work together."

I smiled at that. It was the speech that my heart wanted to hear.

"Sounds good to me," Manny grinned like a child who's had too much candy on Halloween. I think everyone was smiling.

"Same here," Gran offered. "So let's get at it! This is what the Prophecy says." She took a deep, steady breath, and I watched as her stomach filled up and let go of the air.

"And so it begins,
The quest of Shifters,
A Guardian, the youngling,
Someone who is not who they seem
A great war coming,
Who will harness the Full Elemental Power
A son of Fire will decide
Betrayal from a leader
Bold blood will be shed,
And one nearly visits the dead."

I shivered. Dada scratched his wild beard. "Let's just say I do not like the sound of the last line."

"Or the second to last," Mama added.

"Or the third to last, or the fourth to last," I said glumly. "This whole Prophecy isn't sounding too good. And I still don't get why I'm the Guardian."

"You're the youngling. Duh." Eleanor rolled her eyes, sparking something inside me.

"But-"

"Just be grateful," she snapped.

Right then, I recognized something in her voice, something sharp and barbed. I found myself replying with the first thing that came to my mind. "If I didn't know better, I'd think you were jealous!" I remarked angrily. My insides churned, annoyance snapping at me hungrily.

Eleanor looked ready to burst, but Mama gave a sharp whistle. Everyone jumped. "That's enough," she warned, her eyes a mix of heartbreak and fierce anger. "I don't like these little disagreements at all." Her voice was filled with disappointment and iciness. "You two better shape up."

"And if you guys continue acting like anything other than sisters . . ." Dada let the sentence hang threateningly in the humid air.

We both stayed achingly silent. I felt the shame washing over me, like the tide, but when the water pulled back, I still felt mad. I wanted her to be the Guardian, not me! Yet that's who she was mad at. Me. I secretly wondered if there could have been another youngling out there who was younger than me. Was I really the one for the job?

We walked back to the parking lot, drowning in deep silence. The shame still brewed inside me. I didn't want to tear my family apart. Well, Eleanor was the one who left, so . . . But I whipped my head crossly. Sisters. I tried to think determinedly, but shakiness trickled in. Sisters. I thought again, my eyes welling up.

Beside me, Manny walked in his old-and-wise person way. It surprised me when he placed a wrinkled hand on my shoulder. Suddenly I wanted to pour my heart to the old man who'd just organized my ritual. Instead I held back and whispered. It took a lot.

"What if I can't do it?"

My voice felt weak and was trembling. Inside my head, I decided on an answer. Don't worry, you'll not only let your family down but also all the Wind Shifters. Oh, wait, actually, the whole Wind Nation. And lose the Great War. No biggie!

"It's in the Prophecy, dear." Manny talked about as calmly as I wished I was.

"I know, but . . ." I sighed, feeling ready to sob. Still I kept my voice low, for some reason this was easier to talk to Manny about. Although I didn't know him until tonight. "The Prophecy, what if, well, it doesn't work? That's happened before, right? And it's not like it'll make me magically braver and successful."

Manny paused thoughtfully, seeming to collect his thoughts. "Well, I think you already have that bravery. Right here," he smiled and pointed to my heart. "I think maybe that courage is just a tad bit shy. How about that?"

"Okay," I said, a smile twitching at my lips. "But, Manny, how do I make my bravery braver?" I asked, feeling silly. It almost sounded like we were speaking in tongues.

"Honestly, that's up to you," Manny said very seriously. "I know you can do it, Blair. I mean, Shifting is probably the first step to getting bravery out of its shell." I giggled and he continued, "And, I have to say, your gran's prophecies are never wrong." He winked mischievously. "Don't tell her I said so."

I smiled. He and Gran were pretty alike, I guessed. Then I realized something . . . Did Manny like Gran? I played with the thought amusedly. I was too tired to make up my mind, but it was possible. Since I'd never seen Grandpa, it didn't particularly bother me, as long as he was good to her. Plus, Manny seemed nice. I grinned up at him, and it felt like I knew a secret.

"Okay. Thanks, and good luck."

Manny seemed confused. "With what, dear? That's what I was going to say to you, actually . . ." He was so clueless I laughed, making everyone stare. We'd reached our car. When everyone else had climbed in, I leaned toward him and whispered. "You two are perfect for each other. His cheeks flushed with bright color. Inwardly I chuckled, and as I climbed into the back seat, I felt a tiny bit better.

Chapter 13. Still Sisters

The next morning it was dark when I woke up. It was too early to wake, I knew, but I didn't try to sleep more. Eleanor was snoring loudly beside me. Longingly I stared at her. I didn't want to fight anymore; it felt like I'd had a revengeful storm inside me before, but now it had slowed to a drizzle. It just seemed like we needed a final touch to bring the sun out. Something big, super good sisterly bonding experience.

A funny thought jumped into my head. The Great War . . . perfect for sisterly bonding! I knew it was something I shouldn't joke about, but it was kind of funny.

I got ready for the day as if I had all the time in the world. I couldn't believe that because of the heat we had no school. It was Thursday! We should have started school four days ago. Yet I did not want to think about school right now; I had way too much already going on.

Waking up early was nice. It gave me cherished time to be alone with just me and my thoughts. Being in a big family, sometimes I needed that. I scoured every inch of my memories, searching for some sort of clue about who the spy was.

Most of all, I went over everything that happened at the ritual. A lot of it wasn't pretty, but there was one thing that kept haunting me - that voice that came into my head before I Shifted. It sounded so familiar but also so . . . not.

Soon, child, you, your family and your whole House will be sucked into my trap.

I shivered. I could still hear the voice echoing in my head. It sounded jolly but the words were absolutely terrifying. What trap? I wanted to scream at it. And how? Who are you anyway?

I waited, but of course it didn't answer me. For one, though, the voice sounded female. That was a start. Maybe it could have been Imogen? I considered it. Was the voice British, like hers? I did remember thinking that her voice didn't match her vibe. That cheery voice did not complement her cold teal eyes.

I wondered if Imogen could Shift. Back at the ritual, Eleanor said people with teal eyes were Fire Shifters. That would mean Hudson could Shift, too.

The more I thought, the more I felt certain that Hudson could Shift.

A lot of things are difficult, he'd said. *You know, it'll figure itself out. Things will get easier, I promise. I know! Sure, it's different, and strange, and . . . well.*

That's what he said to me. It sounded like he knew I Shifted, promising and saying things were difficult. But then, was he the enemy? The vicious spy who was giving away all our inside information was a thirteen-year-old boy? My head hurt from thinking, and just when I was about to give up, Eleanor woke up.

She didn't say anything as she sat down next to me. Her hair was weaved into thick braids, but they were frizzed up from sleep.

"Good morning," I said softly.

"Morning."

"You're up early," I said.

"So are you," she countered. Her voice was brisk.

"Yeah, but-" I stopped myself before finishing, *you usually sleep in.* I had a feeling it wasn't a good idea to talk with Eleanor before eight o'clock, especially when we'd had a huge fight just last night.

"Any plans today?" Eleanor asked, her calmness regained, though I still felt I was skating on thin ice.

"No," I just answered politely.

She looked at me, her face contorted. It screamed, what am I ever going to do with you? "I swear, Blair," she said, bitterness tucked away, "when you grow up, you should hire a life planner. Otherwise I don't know how you'll ever remember things.

My anger spiked up at the comment. I couldn't tell if it was a joke or not, but either way it was rude. I was about to protest when she interrupted, "Kidding. But I really thought you'd remember today."

"What's today?" I asked, searching my brain. Her birthday?

"Wow, girl. Your first date, silly!" Dreamily, she smiled. "Although your 'date' might be the enemy. Crazy coincidences, huh? I wonder if someday we'll piece it together, what really went down. After we win the war, of course."

"Oh, right," I said, embarrassed. "Eleanor, it's not a date. He's so annoying, always so smug . . ." my voice trailed off. "I'm just being a good neighbor. Like anyone would."

"Sure, sure," Eleanor teased.

"Really, I don't," I groaned.

"If you say so. Anyway." (Subject change.) "When are you going over to his house?" she questioned. I considered this quickly.

"I don't think I'm going to his house," I said. "That'd be super weird, since I don't really know him."

"Plus he's the enemy," she added, and I frowned.

"I don't think he is," I muttered.

"What?" Eleanor's eyebrows jumped up, settling high on her

bronze forehead. "Of course they're the enemy. I mean, it's kind of obvious. The teal eyes, blonde curly hair, pale skin, strange personalities."

"Okay, Imogen's creepy, but Hudson's not," I jutted in.

Her eyes narrowed. "There you go again, defending him. You just don't want to accept that he's evil because one, you're madly in love with him, and two, you hate all my ideas."

I felt sick and broken, slightly nauseous. I didn't hate all Eleanor's' ideas, I thought miserably. But with the way I've been acting? I felt terrible . . . just like I did when she left us. I guess I was still holding a grudge, but that was only because I loved her. It's not a good feeling when someone you love leaves.

"Eleanor," I whispered, dragging out a pause. "I'm really sorry. I don't hate your ideas, they're amazing. They're so amazing, I get jealous. A- and you're right. I don't want to accept that the Ignis' are evil-"

"Except for Imogen, because she's just creepy."

"-because I think Hudson is a good person, and-"

"You're madly in love with him?" Smugly, she cut in. I think I saw a hint of a smile overcome her face.

"No, let me finish!" I complained, giggling. I tried for seriousness again. "I was hurt when you left us. I didn't know why at the time, and it felt like you were leaving us behind. Wearing contacts, not answering our calls, moving away . . . and you didn't even care." I hated my voice for breaking at the last part.

Eleanor's eyes watered. "You've got it all wrong," she said brokenly. "I cared so much, Blair. The thought of you guys hurt so bad, I had to shut it out. I hated school at first; it was just a horrific reminder that I missed my family, my home, with all my heart.

"And so I decided to close out all thoughts of you. Now I know it was wrong, but it was because I loved you. You don't know what it's been like, after missing you all that time, I come back and you hate me."

Now we were both crying. "I don't hate you, Eleanor," I choked out, leaning against her. I hugged her tight, and she hugged back.

"I told you, call me Ellie." We smiled, and I could practically feel the love pouring in between us. It felt so good to have my big sister back.

Chapter 14. Date?

I fiddled with my dark hair. For once it wasn't frizzy; Ellie had used up almost a whole can of hairspray on it. On the base of my neck was an artfully messy bun, with two curled pieces falling from it. It looked too good to be true.

My hair offered to me a slightest bit of extra bravery, making me look ready. Truly, I knew that despite my hair, my favorite jean skirt and white blouse, and the lip gloss that Ellie gave me, I knew I'd never be ready to see Hudson.

Yet I had to try.

Uncertainly, I held my hand out and knocked on the huge door. Everything about Hudson's house was imitating. The door, for one, was. It was dark maroon, more than twice my height. It also had a big, shimmery brass knocker, but for some reason, I just knocked.

A stranger opened the door. She had washed out red hair and almost translucent skin. She looked bored, with her flat features. She also wore a black and white apron, which made me think she was a maid. I'd never seen one before; it seemed like something queens and kings had.

"Hi. Is Hudson here?" My words were quiet.

"Over there, down 'em hallway and to the left. You can't miss 'em," she grumbled, her words careless and annoyed sounding.

I offered a rushed, "Thanks," before zipping down the hallway she'd pointed at . . . and the door on the left . . . yes, this was Hudson's room. Obviously, I thought, reading the sign hanging from a door. It said:

HUDSON'S ROOM
DO NOT ENTER.

I swallowed hard at the huge, blocky letters. Then I rolled my eyes at myself. Oh, come on, I thought, I'm not really scared, am I?

I decided not to answer that question. I knocked gingerly. No answer. Again, I rapped hard on the pristine, white door. "Maybe I'll take a tiny peek . . ." I muttered. I didn't want Hudson to think I was a bad neighbor.

I opened the door after a deep breath. And there was Hudson.

He was sprawled across his bed looking like a model. His hair was splayed all over his pillow, sparkling in the light of the window above his bed. I spotted AirPods jammed into his ears, which had explained why he hadn't heard me knocking. His head bobbed violently to whatever music he was listening to, and that's when I noticed it:

He was crying.

Not sobbing, but silent tears dropped from his face. Instantly I felt terrible for coming in uninvited, and I jerked back just to stumble into the door. It made a loud noise, and Hudson gasped. There was surprise in his huge, teal eyes, and he looked like he'd seen a ghost.

"I-um, what are you doing here?" Hudson sputtered, his cheeks as red as the shirt he was wearing. I'm sure mine were three times as bright.

I wished I could go back in time. "Sorry!" I yelped, feeling helpless. "I'll just go," I smiled, but it didn't reach my eyes. I was about to close the door when Hudson jumped up.

"Wait." He looked at me long enough to make me squirm. It felt like he was looking into my soul. Hudson cleared his throat and rubbed his eyes. If I didn't know he was just crying, I'd think nothing more of the motion. "Why are you here, anyway?"

My cheeks were starting to burn me, they were so red. "Because at dinner. You said-"

"If we wanted to meet up sometime. If you wanted to show me around," Hudson finished tiredly. It was the first time he didn't sound confident or smug when we talked. "And today's Thursday, isn't it?" He spoke the words not totally in question form like he should've, but as a bland statement.

"Yes," I said carefully. "But if today's not a good day, we can do it later-" I began to promise, but Hudson interrupted.

"Nah, today's perfect." And the smugness was spot on, also.

"Okay," I smiled awkwardly, just standing there. "So . . . what's with the sign? And your mood?" I teased, but instantly I knew I shouldn't.

"Two words," Hudson said darkly. "My mom." His Caribbean-blue eyes looked like a storm had overcome them. "She's not good news, Blair. Please stay away from her," he said in a low, warning voice.

With a chill, I wondered if he could mean that she was the spy. "What kind of bad?" I whispered, worrying I was pushing too far. Hudson just shook his curls, pushing them in front of his eyes.

"I can't say." My heart dropped with disappointment at his words. This was crucial stuff. "Hey, but probably better than you're thinking. I mean, look at your face," he added, and snickered.

I rolled my eyes, secretly happy for the subject change.

Hudson continued on, still laughing. "Did you think she was an assassin or something? That she was planning a war?" He burst out laughing. But I sucked in a breath. His 'guesses' had come way too close to reality.

"You okay there?" Hudson asked. "You just got, like, super pale."

"Fine."

"Sure, sure. Anyway, welcome to my house," Hudson smiled jokingly. I laughed as I took it all in. Yet as I glanced around me, Hudson's room didn't look anything like how I imagined it. I thought the walls would be some bright color, and there'd be a bunch of sarcastic posters hung up. Maybe there would be a huge window view and a king size bed. Oh, and some cozy, warm lamps. Basically, I imagined Hudson's room would be cool, and modern . . .

But it wasn't like that at all.

The walls were the whitest of white, and the overhead lights reminded me of hospital ones; blaring and bleak. In the corner, there was a boring, dusty, wooden desk. It looked unused. And last, his bed. It was simple and perfectly made. I stared at the room I was in and noticed it had nothing personal. No photos, no drawings. It made my heart break for the beautiful boy who stood in front of me, fidgeting nervously.

"I'm sorry," I said. I resisted the urge to hug him, because that would be weird. I wasn't sure he'd get why I was saying sorry, but he did. Sadly, he looked at me.

"Don't be," he assured me, but his voice cracked. "Now, what are we waiting for?"

"Pretty sure I'm waiting for you."

Hudson grinned, his confidence roaring back. "Right."

Soon, we were back outside, and it felt great. We casually talked, teasing each other and throwing some snarky comments around. I showed him some nice features of the neighborhood, like the park. And although he'd already seen the creek a bunch of times, we went again because it was so fun. Playfully, we splashed the cool water at each other and skipped the smooth stones we found. It didn't work too well with the current, but we tried anyway.

Finally I skipped a rock and got three hops. Our record previously was two. "Ha, in your face," I stuck out my tongue and wiggled my fingers.

"Oh, come on," Hudson groaned. "Who knew Miss Perfect Pants could be so cocky?" His hair glowed and his eyes twinkled as he finished smugly, "Just watch this." Hudson picked up a huge, moss-covered rock and tossed it into the river, creating a gigantic splash. We were drenched now.

"Argh! Why did you have to do that?" I said, trying to be pouty, but soon we were both uncontrollably laughing. I felt bad for Eleanor when I remembered the hour she'd spent on my hair. It was now a soaking mess. When we both stopped laughing, I smiled longingly. I wished I could stay here forever, far away from my drama and duties as the Guardian. And yet . . .

"I should probably get back soon."

I hated those words from coming out of my mouth. Hudson sighed. "Ugh. Me too. Back to my boring little house with Mommy Dearest," he said sarcastically. His eyes got stormy again, and I stared sadly at him. He had it pretty hard. "Sorry, sorry," he groaned, and I jumped.

"Uh, for what?"

He offered a lopsided smile. "It's not your fault. I just hate when people feel sorry for me, like I'm some poor little animal," he said, his cheeks reddening.

"Hey, I wasn't looking at you like that!" I protested, rolling my eyes. He raised an eyebrow, not saying anything. "What? I wasn't. I was actually thinking that you must be pretty tough," I admitted. Then I realized how that sounded and blushed. "I mean-"

"I get it, Blair," Hudson said, eyes dancing as his mouthed curved into a grin.

"Not like that!" I yelled behind me as I dashed away. Right before I reached the underbrush, I turned around. "I can't stand you, Hudson Ignis. But I know I'll see you soon," I smiled and raced through the bushes, listening to the delightful sound of Hudson's laughter echo throughout our creek.

Chapter 15. We Strategize

"So, how did it go?" Ellie sang, right when I got home. She had been waiting for me.

"Good." I giggled, fighting the urge to twirl with happiness.

"Just 'good'?" Ellie complained, taking my shoulders and shaking them playfully. "Come on, girl! I'm your sister. Give me the details."

I sigh-smiled. Then I graced over everything we did. "I went to his house," I told her, shyly tucking a strand of hair behind my ear.

"Wait, what? You told me you weren't going to. You said that it would be super weird, since you didn't really know him," Ellie accused, but she was grinning smugly. "What happened to that, huh?"

"Nothing," I said back. "There was just no other way to get to him, and . . . yeah."

"Okay," sang Ellie. "Tell me more, tell me more!" she chanted giddily. So I told her all about his house, but skipped over the crying part. It seemed too personal. Then I went over the places I took him. Ellie waited patiently, listened with a dreamy smile painted on her face. Of course, she did cut in once or twice.

"And what happened to your hair?" she inquired once.

"Oh, yes," I said sheepishly. "We were splashing each other in the creek, being ridiculous."

Ellie squealed. "Tell me about that!" And I continued on. During the explanation, Ellie murmured something that sounded like, "splash-flirting." I blushed. That was when the rest of our family walked in.

"Blair!" Dada boomed.

"Where've you been all day?" Mama said playfully, though I was sure Ellie had already told her.

"You were with that boy of yours, weren't you?" Gran was all smiles as she tousled my damp hair.

"My double agent!" Dada smiled, and patted the couch space next to him. "Now, tell me everything." Double agent? Did they think I was just spying on Hudson the whole time? I hadn't even thought about that.

Dazed, I tried to keep smiling. "Well," I cleared my throat, "Hudson was pretty good at hiding the good information." I fake-smiled. After a pause, Gran concluded:

"So you didn't learn anything?"

Everyone looked crestfallen. I was about to try to lighten the mood when Monnie and Luna walked up, Atticus in between them. They held his tiny, chubby hands as he took a few wobbly steps. "Look at Atticus, Mama! He's walking!" Luna cheered. The sight was so adorable everyone clapped along and said, "Go Atticus!" I was also glad for the subject change.

After that incident, the younger kids went to go play outside. Mama leaned forward and whispered to Ellie and I as they dashed outside, "War strategy meeting. Come to the living room."

My heart sped up.

Our living room looked completely transformed. The two big leather couches and chairs had been pushed to the side, and so had the coffee table to make room for a long, giant foldable table. The cozy, homey feeling it always possessed had vanished.

There were also so many people.

A lot of people looked familiar, and I guessed it was because of the ritual the other night. I spotted Manny and that freckled face girl in the crowd. Despite the amount of people, the room was quiet. Maybe that's why I jumped when Gran clapped her hands, and everyone took a seat.

"Welcome to the strategizing session. Time is precious and mustn't be wasted. Thank you. And all ideas will be shared at the end." Gran was grim and brisk; even her silver hair didn't glitter in the light like usual.

People started hissing and whispering to each other. They grouped up and discussed matters; one that I overheard was discussing possible allies, another was talking about a rally and weapons. Quickly I pushed through the crowd to Mama and Dada.

"-not enough time," I heard someone saying. I walked up to Mama and tugged her hand before grabbing it. The girl they were talking to, the one with the freckles, looked me over.

"Avery, meet our daughter, Blair," Dada introduced, but he sounded kind of rushed. "Blair, this is Avery, a friend of ours." He gave me a warning look, but I didn't know why.

"Hi."

"Blair, is it? I've heard much," Avery said mysteriously. Her freckled face twitched. "But you're so young. Are you prepared to be our Guardian? To protect our power source? Are you prepared for the war?" she asked intensely.

"I-um, I don't really know," I stuttered, freaking out as her eyes bored into mine.

"No one is." She sighed dramatically. "Why did they move it up a few days?" Avery shook her head disapprovingly.

I whipped my head around, confusion injecting into my bones. "Move it up?" I gasped. "What's she talking about?" My heart hammered against my ribs.

"The Fire people are moving faster than we realized. Last night,

Gran looked into the future and . . . well, they're coming much quicker than expected." Dada's voice attempted to be light and even, but even I could detect the fear in it.

So many questions swarmed me. But my voice didn't seem to work. "When?" was all I could choke out. I didn't think anyone would understand the one-worded, vague question, but Mama pulled me in.

"Two days," she whispered, and I wanted to scream and hide and cry. Mostly hide. Because I knew this wasn't a game. That my life was on the line. That I should be doing everything I can to not only protect myself, along with my family and the whole Wind Nation.

But I wasn't.

So despite my butterfly-filled stomach, my head that hurt from worry, and stronger-than-a-tornado feelings, I had to get my act together.

And I had two days.

"Yes, she's young. But very brave," Manny said, joining our conversation. He wore a long maroon robe, and with his long white beard, he looked even more like a sun-tanned Dumbledore. "Celeste and Cameron here told me she went over to the spy's house today. What a double agent!" He smiled warmly at me. People *ooh*ed and *ahh*ed with approval.

But I wasn't being a double agent, I thought, filled with shame. *I was hanging out with Hudson. Playing in the creek,* I thought again. *I'm not going to accept that Hudson's the enemy,* I promised to myself.

Soon, everything was whipped into a plan. We'd meet early at the top of a hill, to get high ground. Ironically, the hill was called the Gods' Gateway. "It's so tall and impressive, in the old days mortals went there to pray because they believed it would bring them closer to the gods."

"Then why are we fighting there?" I asked. "If it's so sacred and religious, why are we having the Great War at the Gods' Gateway?" It sounds like fantasy, I thought. Eleanor nodded in agreement.

Manny's wrinkled round face was grave as he answered. "We'll need all the blessings we can get for this," he said. "And like we stated before, it's the higher ground."

"Got it."

We didn't know what time they'd arrive at Gods' Gateway, to battle, but Gran said that in her vision, the sun was vertical in the sky. So maybe mid-day? But that was the tricky part about this. Somehow the spy had informed the Fire Nation that we had a Teller. So they were being careful about not setting things in stone. It was annoying. Somehow the spy had also informed the Fire Nation that we were going to fight.

Hudson just *couldn't* be the spy. That was my only thought.

For weapons, we didn't have too many. But our most powerful one would be Shifters. Me. Eleanor. All the people from Birming Dale. "We have more Shifters than the Fire Nation. It's one of our only advantages,"

Mama said, a glint in her eyes. I translated it to, *we're all depending on you. If we lose, the Fire Nation will have Full Elemental Power. They'd be unstoppable. So no pressure.*

I thought of what Gran had said when I asked what Full Elemental Power was. "Bad," she'd said. "Extremely bad. Us, the Wind Nation would lose the ability to Shift. And while we lose our power, their power would amplify twenty times greater than it was before."

I shivered. No way I was going to let that happen. But I kind of felt like I needed some sort of training. I mean, I had only Shifted twice but I was expected to protect, oh, I don't know, one hundred people?

That's why I came to Ellie and asked her if she would train me. I pulled her away from a debate and asked her, "Will you teach me how to Shift?"

"You already know how."

"No, not like that," I said irritably. "You know what I mean. Will you train me? So I can be a better Shifter," I explained.

Ellie considered, contemplating long enough to make me itch. "I doubt we'll have enough time. And I've only been at Birming Dale for a month, you know. I don't think-" I cut her off.

"Please, Ellie?" I begged, on my wits end. "I'll feel terrible if . . . if someone . . ." my voice failed. "And it was my fault. I'd have to live the rest of my life knowing that I didn't truly do everything I could," I said hoarsely.

Ellie's look softened. "I'm sorry," she sighed. "Of course I'll train you."

"You don't sound too eager," I pointed out, only half teasing. She shook her head doubtfully.

"Oh, shut up," she said, skipping toward our parents. "Let's go see if we can. I know the perfect place."

Chapter 16. Practice Makes Perfect

"It's . . . open," I offered unsurely, staring at the huge field around me. Although it was closed in by tall, thick, trees, the field was about as big as a baseball one. The grass was long and very naturally pretty. Above me, the sun shined and the blue sky seemed bigger than usual.

"Pretty neat, in my opinion," Ellie replied, smiling. She propped her bike up against a moss-covered tree. I followed and propped mine next to hers; we'd biked here from home. The ride really wasn't far, on the contrary, it was scenic and wow-inducing.

"Ready?" she asked, then without hesitation spirited forward. "Race you to the middle of the field!" she called behind her. Despondent, I sighed. But I was smiling as I raced after her.

Ellie didn't say anything when I caught up to her, but she triumphantly grinned. She didn't have to brag; her eyes said everything. Yet in a flash she was firm. "First, we Shift," she instructed.

"But how will we talk to each other?" I wondered.

"Just Shift!" The edge in her voice convinced me. This time, I didn't even have to think about being angry or upset. I just closed my eyes and embraced my spirit self. Prayers and encouragement flowed through my head as soon as I did.

Ooh. Sissy bonding.
Third time's the charm, dearie.
You go, girl!

A part of me wished I would hear Hudson's voice in my head. Saying, *you got it, Blair.* Smooth, confident, warm . . . But of course I didn't hear it.

When I opened my eyes, Eleanor stood beside me, in dragon form. I stared at her, open mouthed. She was bigger than I was, and a dark, shimmery green. Her scales glittered, the emerald color reminding me of thick forests. *I thought all Wind Shifters were gold!*

Nope. A high, soprano voice echoed throughout my head.

Ellie!? I thought frantically. *Are we . . .*

It's called the spirit mind connection, she explained. *Basically, we can read each other's thoughts.*

Wow. I watched, mesmerized as her emerald tail flicked gracefully. *I can see why you got those green tips in your hair,* I thought quietly. Ellie sniffed.

Yes. Now, let's fly. Ellie spiraled toward the sky, so graceful and perfect.

Show-off! I flapped my big gold wings, and unsteadily I lifted into the air. The wind was naughty, shoving and pushing me off balance. It really wasn't easy to fly; I couldn't seem to hover and I had to flap my wings really fast to stay steady.

How are you so good at this? I asked, strained. My wings ached, but when I glanced at Ellie she was effortlessly spinning and curving. Ellie only bared her teeth, but I think she was trying to smile. *No, seriously!* I protested. *You have to help me!*

Yeah, yeah, Ellie teased, nudging me. *It's all about finding the wind. If you know how strong it is, and which way it's going, then it's easy. Of course you also just have to practice using your wings.*

Okay, I replied with my thoughts.

Want to know a trick?

Um, YES, PLEASE.

Ellie nodded her beautiful dragon head. She had a pointed snout that was a shade lighter than the rest of her dark green body, and curly horns protruding from it. She looked so serene and smart and magical; it was impossible not to be jealous.

Your tail, she answered, and I could see her mind flash to a field bigger than this one. The grass was trimmed perfectly and behind there was a huge stony castle. Birming Dale, I recognized quickly. A plump teacher paced in front of the students, and suddenly I recognized her too.

Mrs. Plia? I thought.

That's her, Ellie answered, making me jump. *Forgot I was here, did you?* she teased.

Maybe, I replied distantly, focused on the memory. Mrs. Plia spoke in that peppy voice of hers, all cheerful. It reminded me of something, but I couldn't put my finger on it. "Welcome to your first Shifting lesson," she was saying, "Today we're going to practice flying. Very exciting for all you huns, I'm sure, but more difficult than you'd realize." I caught the wink she tossed over her shoulder. "Now, hun, the trick to flying is quite simple, really. All you've got to do is feel with your tail. Now, now, don't give me that look! Your tail will instinctively feel the wind, so just look behind you and it'll point the way the wind's blowing. Then you can figure out traction and physics, and it's unbelievably easier."

But I don't know about traction and physics, I complained.

That's not important. Ellie shooed the comment away. *Translated from teacher talk, all she's saying is that you have to go with Mother Nature. You can't fight the wind. It will always be stronger than you. But if you go with it . . . well, you would be unstoppable.*

A warm, inspired feeling sparked inside. I realized I was . . . excited! *Atta girl.* I could practically hear the smile in Ellie's voice. *Remember I can read your thoughts,* she mocked. I rolled my gold eyes.

I called back what Mrs. Plia had told Ellie. "All you've got to do is feel with your tail." Her voice was high and smiley . . .

I inhaled sharply. My heart pounded and my stomach churned.

Uh, what's going on? Ellie said nervously. *Your thoughts are speeding really fast, I can't even read them!*

I-I . . . I sputtered. *I knew it! I knew Hudson wasn't the spy!* I would've been grinning if I could.

Will you please explain to me what is going on? Ellie demanded.

It's a long story but . . .

We've got time.

I stopped myself from protesting that two days was barely any time at all. *When I was Shifting at the ritual, I heard a voice in my head. Most of the voices are nice. One said "Happy ritual" and another said "Congrats." But there was one . . .* I shivered. *I knew the voice was so familiar. It was all smiley and peppy. But you know what it said?* My voice shook.

What? Ellie's thoughts were almost silent. I took a deep breath before going on.

The cheerful voice told me, "Soon, child, you, your family and your whole House will be sucked into my trap." But I didn't know who said it.

When Ellie jerked back with astonishment, it sent a gust of wind hurtling toward me. *That's . . . that's really scary. Terrible. Why didn't you tell me?*

I pretended to not hear the catch in her voice. *There was just so much going on, with the war and everything . . . But that voice. I knew I knew it from somewhere.*

And let me guess. Ellie's voice was broken and faded. Her gold dragon eyes flickered around. *The voice belonged to Mrs. Plia. And when you saw my memory, you realized.*

Pretty much, I said, dispirited.

Now that I think of it, Ellie continued, her voice the picture of dread, *it makes total sense if she's the spy. She's so nice. Even though she teaches Shifting, she's basically a guidance counselor for all of Birming Dale. People tell her everything!* Her wings flapped anxiously. *I mean everything! She knows the drama, the news, the secrets.*

I took a shuddery breath. *We need to tell Mama and Dada and Gran and Manny.* I finished the thought before I could go on forever. (The whole Wind Nation).

Good idea. Let's Shift back.

I nodded and let the tingly feeling wash over myself. Before I knew it Ellie was standing next to me. She was stone-faced, her dark hair flowing behind her with the wind. I almost didn't hear her as she whispered, "I can't believe Mrs. Plia would do something like that."

My stomach jumped. "You're sure, right?" she breathed. "Totally sure?"

"Positive." My grim voice seemed to be absorbed by the spacious field. It felt weird to speak aloud again.

Ellie just nodded, a faraway look in her eyes as we walked away from the field and to our bikes. I didn't seem to have the energy to pedal all the way back home, but I scraped enough up and off we went.

Chapter 17. Spies

My breath wobbled in and out shakily. There were so many emotions pounding in my head, and most of them I didn't have a name for. One of the easier ones to decipher was pure fear. I was going to be in a war. *The Great War*, I thought, the words claiming an ominous feel. I could die. But part of me was also . . .

Intrigued?

No, that seemed wrong. I don't think there was a word for it. Of course I wasn't intrigued to fight in a war. But a small part of me held tight to a strange fascination. There were three Houses going to be there. And Shifters with their dragons! It felt like a fantasy.

And of course I was overcome with steely determination. *We were going to win. And I'm going to protect everyone.* Those words chorused on and on in my head; *We're going to win. And I'm going to protect everyone . . .*

I was sitting at the fold-up table that was currently invading my living-room. All the people had left, probably because it was seven o'clock. We'd just finished dinner, so now it was time.

Ellie and I agreed to tell them after dinner that Mrs. Plia was the spy. I knew Ellie was upset about it, and we both needed time to process, but I couldn't put off the news forever.

It was time.

"Okay, go ahead and tell us why Ellie's got those worry creases all over her forehead and you're as pale as a Fire Shifter." Gran, warm and blunt as ever.

"Mom!" Mama reprimanded. But she too searched our faces, seeking answers that weren't there. I glanced at Ellie. *You want to say something? Or should I?* How I wished she could read my thoughts right now.

"We think Mrs. Plia is the spy." I decided to get the words out of my mouth before I could overthink it.

Dada didn't try to hide his confusion. "Who's Mrs. Plia?"

"The teacher from Visiting day," Mama murmured thoughtfully. "Why do you think that, girls?"

Ellie took over the story then. "When Blair was Shifting at the ritual . . ." During her explanation there were many interruptions, varying from gasps to "Why didn't you tell us?"" Finally Ellie finished the story. After a few beats of silence, she spoke up again.

"It makes perfect sense, doesn't it?" She tilted her head

thoughtfully. "She knows everything."

"It does, doesn't it?" Mama replied, equally as compelled. "But what about the Ignis'? They still make sense too. Blonde curls, teal eyes, super pale. They fit the role exactly."

"I'm not saying that they're not part of the Fire Nation," I pushed. "But I still don't think that they are *spies*." The last word in my sentence sounded like a curse. "They just moved here. How could they have found out everything about us? Mrs. Plia, on the other hand, has worked at Birming Dale for years. Probably listened when her students told her they were going to war with the Fire Nation, right?"

Everyone absorbed my words with an eerie silence. Finally Manny shattered it. "My, you've grown up since last I talked to you!" He smiled, and the rest of my family followed his lead.

"She sure has," Ellie grinned, punching my arm. "You think you're ready?"

I stood up. "Let's go kick some Fire Nation butt." We all cheered and high-fived. Then Dada shooed us away.

"Go get ready for bed, my big girls. You've got a big two days coming up!"

"Aw, come on, Dada!" we both complained, holding on to each other. "It's seven-forty-five! And we've got so much energy!" We giggled and jumped up and down.

"Then you can go and play with Monnie and Luna and Atticus. They're in the playroom," Gran added, her face lit up with mischievousness and glee. "They are sure to tire anyone out with that imagination of theirs."

"You've got us there," Ellie teased, and we walked away.

After we brushed our teeth and put on our pajamas, and Ellie put her hair into braids, we entered the playroom. Our little siblings looked adorable, and get this; they were all wearing matching onesie pajamas. Luna's dark hair and eyes shone, Monnie's face was lit up and Atticus's round face was mischievous and lovely. I ruffled his random brown tufts of hair as I sat down and pulled him onto my lap.

"Can we play, too?" Ellie asked, almost smug. We knew they'd be jumping with joy and squealing happily.

"Yeah! Play with us! Play with us!" Luna yelled, her grin seeming too big for her smooth, round face. Monnie giggled, and hypnotized by their love, I did too. It felt good to be the older ones for a change, the ones who were looked up to.

It was crazy to think that by this time tomorrow we would know who won the war - or we might still be fighting in it.

"You can be the good dragon," Monnie bossed, "Because Atticus is already the bad dragon. 'Because he likes to destroy the castles," she explained. Ellie and I smiled sadly at each other. Once again, her games had touched down too close to reality.

"Me and Luna are the princesses." She smiled, pleased. "You guys have to protect us, okay?"

"Got it," I whispered. I looked into everyone's eyes, and promised them all something I knew that only Ellie would understand. "I promise to protect you all," I said seriously, my heart thudding with pride, determination and bravery. "Whatever happens, I'll be there." I hugged my little siblings and my big sister fighting back tears. After a few beats of comfortable silence, Luna squirmed.

"I thought you said you would *play*." Luna looked at me innocently, pronouncing her words slow and clear the way my parents sometimes talked to Atticus. I laughed, a deep belly laugh.

"I did!" I protested. "Let's play."

So we did. When it was time for bed, Monnie, Luna and Atticus danced off. Ellie and I talked for a while in our beds, but avoided the topic of the war. It was nice to escape reality, but we'd have to come crawling back eventually.

"Good night," I whispered finally, and tried to sleep.

Chapter 18. What Do I Wear?

The day before the war (or, the Great War Eve, as Ellie was calling it) passed so quickly it was hard to fathom. The whole day blurred into preparations and rallying. Gran helped us find out that the Earth Nation had allied themselves with the Fire Nation.

"They're really just a bunch of lunkheads who do the dirty work," Gran had told me. "Dummies with no mind of their own. Loyal servants who happen to be strong as heck. Perfect allies to beat up their master's enemies."

And the Water Nation was still neutral. At least we and the other Houses agreed on one thing about them; they were mysterious and suspicious. But *they* wouldn't be at the Great War, and that's all I was focused on at the moment.

I rested most of the day, and so did Ellie. Dada said all Shifters were doing so, but I wondered if he was just saying that. Yet I wished so badly I could help. I even begged. "You're already doing enough," was Dada's gruff answer, his face creasing.

And despite that long, suspenseful day, it was now time for the Great War. Today would be the day we found out whether or not the Fire Nation would become the dominant House, the House that harnessed Full Elemental Power.

My alarm clock let out a scream at exactly six o'clock in the morning. The sound immediately sent goosebumps to my skin. I hadn't slept at all, for a single fact pounded its way into my dreams and subconscious and sleep.

The Great War is coming.

Ellie, sleeping next to me, groaned. "Turn that thing off," she murmured, her voice thick with sleep. "It's the weekend." With a sigh I waited for her to come to her senses.

"What do I wear?" I hissed. I stared hard at my drawers, but nothing seemed quite right.

"I don't have the slightest idea," Ellie said, as she too searched her dresser. "But I know staring at your drawers isn't going to make something magically appear."

Tiredly, I smiled. It was a mix of sadness and worry. Nothing would be the same after this. "It shouldn't really matter, because I'll be a dragon most of the time," I said thoughtfully. "But nothing seems right."

Ellie nodded. "Think our closet has anything?"

"Worth a shot." She pulled the door open and gasped. A smile worked its way onto her face, and it seemed to glow in the early light of morning.

"What is it-" I began to ask, but realized I didn't need to. Ellie stepped aside and I saw what she gaped at. "A uniform?" I said. But then I thought it over. Maybe uniform wasn't the right word. A suit? Whatever it was, I loved it.

It had long pants and a button-up jacket, which were both perfectly pressed. Under was a clean white t-shirt. The whole ensemble looked simple and comfy enough, but I couldn't take my eyes off the jacket. It was a beautiful gold color, not too sparkly but not too boring. The buttons were shining bronze, which complimented the gold.

"I think we've found what we were looking for," Ellie said, half smiling. Her eyes shone, matching the jacket and pants. "It's like they were made for us!" she playfully shook me. I didn't say that they probably were.

Quickly, we changed. Ellie looked beautiful. Her hair was smooth and glossy and her forest green highlights stood out. Her shimmery gold eyes, her bronze skin. "You look really good," I told her.

"Right back at you." Her face glowed when she smiled.

That's when Dada peeked his head in. "You guys ready?" I could hear him trying to be brave. Then he saw us. "Oh my spirits, you two are beautiful," he whispered, his voice choked with love. Ellie and I shared a grin, and then went into a hug.

"I love you guys so much," he whispered, and I could almost hear the downpour of tears that dripped to my head. We held each other tight for a while and when we finally pulled away, we shared a sad smile.

"You're going to be careful out there, got it?" Dada shattered the silence. His voice was teasing and light. I knew his way of coping was hiding behind his jokes.

"Got it," Ellie and I said in sync, giggling slightly.

"Now, come on," Dada said. "Let's go for a drive."

Chapter 18. Gods' Gateway

"It's really not how I imagined it," Ellie said to me for what seemed like the hundredth time. "It's so run down. And the Gods' Gateway is a mound of mud," she complained. I rolled my eyes. She was the only thing keeping my spirits up.

"I know, I know. But by this point, I can't say I'm surprised," I replied. "Everywhere the Wind Nation goes, the ground isn't too pretty."

Ellie laughed. "That's because if we took good care of landscaping, it would be considered honoring the Earth Nation. Quite a scandal that would be."

I tried to match her light tone as I responded. "Indeed it would." But still, Gods' Gateway didn't live up to its name. The hill was actually tall, and pretty steep, but it was slippery with the mud. You'd think it would be magical, like you were floating, and there would be mist, and maybe you could touch the clouds.

But nope!

"At least it's sunny," Ellie offered, twisting her midnight hair as she squinted upward.

"Yeah," I muttered back. But it didn't feel like it should be bright and cheerful out. I mean, if we were having a party, it would be great, but a war? Super fitting.

We waited almost three and a half hours before we spotted them. They marched like robots or aliens, coming over the horizon like a dreadful sunset. "There!" A voice had shrieked, maybe Avery. It was followed by many yells in response, "Where?" "Right there!" "Tiny dots . . ."

The teal and brown dots grew scarily fast. "Think the teal uniforms are the Fire Nation? And the brown uniforms are the Earth Nation?" Ellie asked, her voice soft.

"Bet." My voice sounded cracked.

After what seemed like an eternity, they stood at the bottom of the Gods' Gateway. I waited, not breathing. Were we just going to charge? Should I Shift? Questions buzzed in my head. Luckily, I got my answer in a span of seconds.

"Fire Nation," Gran addressed, her voice ringing out amongst the silence. "Earth. Welcome to the Gods' Gateway, and we hope you're ready to witness hell."

I heard a snort and a couple of laughs from our enemies. A scoff, too. I scowled at them hoping I looked brave. But inwardly I couldn't help feeling the fear. Their troops had to be roughly two times the size of ours, and all looked deadly. They were equipped with swords, knives and lethal looking bows that glinted silver in the light. The Earth Nation in the plain brown uniforms looked like giants next to the Fire Nation, towering twice the height and three times the width of most of our people.

I searched the crowd, my insides twisting up. My thoughts were on a one-way track; *Hudson. Hudson! HUDSON!*

And then I saw him. Oh spirits, no. He really was part of the Fire Nation. A part of the enemy. And he looked so excruciatingly good.

His golden hair literally shined, and his curls were perfect ringlets. His skin was pale but his cheeks were flushed pink. I had memorized his face now; the teal eyes, small freckles, prominent nose. I waited for him to see me, but he seemed far away and serious.

But I didn't see Mrs. Plia.

"Impressive ranks you've got here, Victoria." Instantly, I recognized the icy, British voice as Imogen's. The words sunk heavily into the air, and I watched as everyone glared defensively at each other.

"Thank you, I know," was Gran's prim response. She smiled coldly, a smile I rarely saw come from Gran. It made me shiver.

Imogen mirrored her iciness. "Why don't we work some of this tension off on the battlefield?" she offered, delicately folding her hands. I noticed everyone visibly tense.

"Why not?" Gran looked courageous as she pulled out her hair and let it blow behind her. Her face was stony as her lips moved. I barely caught the word as she said it: "Charge."

Someone Shifted. I heard a pop, and a violet dragon with amethyst colored polka dots rose above the crowd. "Shift!" Ellie yelled, and with a crackle she was her emerald self.

I embraced the tingles that itched across my skin. But no voices filled my head this time. When I opened my eyes, my dragon eyes, I only saw chaos. Dragons roared and spewed fire, while the gigantic Earth Nation people fought with our people who weren't Shifters.

What can I do? I thought desperately, hoping Ellie would answer. Maybe even Avery would be okay . . .

Blair? An astonished voice echoed through my head. But it didn't belong to Ellie or Avery. Instead, the smooth, confident, smug voice was . . . Hudson's. *Yeah, it's me,* thought Hudson. *You're a Shifter? For the Wind Nation?*

Yes, I answered frantically.

Oh my god, how is this happening? Hudson moaned. *You're the enemy. We're having a war! I can't even see you but we're having a conversation with our thoughts.* His mind rapidly went on. *I can't-*

Where are you? I demanded, flapping my wings majestically.

Why? Hudson asked, sounding tortured.

I'm at the top of the Gods' Gateway, I continued, ignoring him. *Come up here!* I didn't care that I was in a war. I needed to see Hudson . . . in his spirit form.

Coming. After a few seconds I saw a dragon soaring toward me. Was it . . . yes. Hudson. He was an azure blue, the exact color of his eyes. His tail was sky blue, pointed and barbed. Small horns jutted from his head. But I couldn't tear my eyes from the Caribbean Sea dragon color. It was so pretty.

Thanks, Hudson said smugly, reminding me that my thoughts were not private. *But gold is way cooler.*

I attempted to dragon-smile. But after a second, I realized what was going on below me. People jabbed and yelled, and some lay on the ground. Most were teal or brown, but . . . *I have to protect them,* I thought, pawing the ground nervously.

Me too, Hudson said. I could hear the anxiousness etched into his voice. *Look, my mom isn't great,* he muttered. *But she's not evil. She just wants the best for the Fire Nation.* I nodded, but my mind flashed to when I saw him crying in his room. And her cold looks, her voice saying, "Impressive ranks you've got here, Victoria," and "Why don't we work some of this tension off on the battlefield?"

Woah, woah, Hudson shook his head frantically. *Get those thoughts out of my head! That's a pretty dark way to view a person, you know. My mom is really just introverted and embarrassed. And stressed.* I watched carefully as he thought of her unpacking moving boxes late into the night. *And the crying . . .* he trailed off.

Never mind thinking it aloud, I told him gently. *I read your thoughts already.*

Hudson shuddered in a breath. *Okay, thanks.* But suddenly he looked up, his azure eyes boring into mine. *I would have told you anyway. It's . . . my father. He died in battle when I was a baby.* Hudson's thoughts were almost silent.

I faltered. What would I ever do without a dad? *I'm sorry.*

He sighed deeply, his thoughts still quiet and shaky. *Isn't it so weird how I miss him, when I don't even remember him? I've heard so many stories about him from my mom, and everybody tells me I have his curls . . .* He trailed off into silence, his head filled with sorrow and grief.

I'm sorry, I said again. *You've gone through so much.* And yet he was still perfect and confident and beautiful.

He looked up sneakily, sniffling. He flashed a small smile. *I heard that, Blair,* he teased. My cheeks turned red; oops. But he continued. *But I do want to say thank you.*

Uh, for what? I wondered, confused. But I was grinning.

Two things, Hudson told me confidently. *One, for being there. I was in a new place, miles from home. But you talked to me. Showed me around. You made me feel . . .* He paused, and I could literally see his thoughts shuffling around to find the right words. *At home,* he finally finished. *I look forward to seeing you every day.*

Really? I said slyly. *Because I thought it was just me.*

Nope, Hudson thought. *Although I hide it pretty well, I like you a lot.*

My cheeks burned so red I wondered if it turned my gold scales maroon. But I cleared my throat and tried to not think about how that sounded. Hudson looked like he was trying to hold back laughter as he continued to the second thing.

Also, for not pitying me. His thoughts were softer this time, shyer.

Pitying you?

Yeah, he elaborated, *like feeling sorry for me.*

I was still confused. *Why would I feel sorry for you?* I asked. *I'm not going to baby you,* I added, half teasing.

Because of my dad, Hudson explained. *Usually when I tell people they throw a giant pity party for me. But you-* he looked up, eyes shining *-didn't. You thought of how strong I was, how I must be so brave to go through so much.*

You are! I thought, lashing my tail. *Don't you think that way, too?* Disbelief bloomed in my head when he hesitated.

Kind of? Hudson tried to shrug, but as a dragon it looked funny. *I don't really know.*

Well then, good thing you have me to think that way for you, I retorted, huffing stubbornly. A smile crept up the teal dragon's lips.

It is, he said.

I nodded decidedly. Soon a silence overcame us, but it was the comfortable type. Except when I glanced below, my thoughts roared up so loudly it was hard to breathe.

People swarmed around, jabbing and slashing. No one had fallen down yet, despite having injuries. No one was dead, I realized with a strange sense of relief. Hudson watched my thoughts.

I don't think they really want to hurt each other, he thought slowly. *No one brought guns. Did you realize that?* Hudson asked thoughtfully.

I actually did. I tilted my head slightly. *No bombs, either. Nothing modern, just swords and bows.*

And us, Hudson reminded. And he was right, we were the deadliest weapon. Except . . .

I don't think I could kill anyone, I thought suddenly, my mental voice silent. *Someone who had a family who loved them, who maybe I would've been friends with.*

I know what you mean, Hudson replied, just as quiet. *I mean, we're friends. Surely everyone else could be, too.*

That's when it came to me. *Hudson,* I began excitedly, *we don't have to fight!*

He stared at me. *Look, I wish our House's weren't enemies, but finishing this war is kind of inevitable.*

No, it isn't, I pushed. *My House is made of completely good people, and none deserve war.* I thought of Manny and my family.

Mine don't either! He argued. *And even though I don't know the Earth Nation too well, I don't think they deserve war.* He swallowed. *No one does.* With sadness I watched him imagine his father, curly haired and smiling gently.

I looked at him. *You're right. And that's exactly why we need to bring these people together.*

Hudson tilted his head. *Remind me why they hate each other so much?* he asked with a smile.

You're the ones trying to get Full Elemental Power, I accused.

His perfect teal face crumbled slightly, and it visibly darkened. *That's not us,* he said seriously. There wasn't a crinkle in his dragon scales. *It's . . . Drusilla Plia.*

He saw my face and grumbled. *You go to Birming Dale, don't you? You think she's the best teacher ever, and she'd be the one you'd go to when you're worried. You had a fight with your parents, you broke up with your boyfriend . . .*

I don't have a boyfriend, I interrupted. Then I felt my cheeks flame. *Go on,* I said awkwardly when he laughed.

He shrugged. *There's not much more,* he told me. *Except that I'm sorry.*

It's fine, I assured him. *By now I'm over the shock. And no, I don't go to Birming Dale. My sister does.*

It was kind of amusing to watch his thoughts slowly piece together my words. *You knew?* he asked, his disbelief obvious. *How did you- she was the spy-*

I mimicked his trademark smirk; finally, I wasn't the clueless one. *I figured it out. You know when you get those voices in your head? When you Shift, all of them say stuff like 'good job' and 'you got this'?*

I hate those, Hudson complained. *Although,* he added, a sneaky smile slipping onto his face, *I did that to you when you first Shifted.*

I narrowed my eyes. *I guessed,* I told him with an eye roll. *But I heard Mrs. Plia's voice at my ritual. And she didn't have anything nice to say.* Uncontrollably, her words came to my head.

Oh spirits. I can see why you don't like us, Hudson said, and I couldn't know if he was being serious. *But other than Drusilla, or Mrs. Plia as you know her, we're all good people.*

I frowned. *But isn't she like . . . your queen?*

I saw Hudson's mind mentally shudder. *Of course not,* he said. *More like an evil master who we have to follow. And she's the greatest Shifter of all time, so if we didn't . . .* He let the sentence hang in the air.

I nudged him, trying to picture the smiley Mrs. Plia as an evil master. I already knew she was different, but I couldn't help but ask. *You're all scared of . . . Mrs. Plia?*

Hudson sighed, lifting off the ground slightly. *You make her sound like a hamster.*

Sorry, but it's hard to picture Mrs. Plia-

He laughed lightly, but I saw how he imagined Mrs. Plia; a cross between Maleficent and a vampire. *Call her Drusilla,* Hudson suggested. *It's so much more fitting.*

I guess it is, I said thoughtfully. *Is that her real name?*

Actually, I'm not sure, Hudson chuckled. I did, too. A beat of silence passed, and I thought about our plan that needed way more planning. *Do you really think they'll listen?* Hudson thought quietly.

My heart leaped at the question, and I glanced below me at the shouting people. *Maybe,* I thought, my mental voice hitching up at the end as if the word was a question. *If we could just convince them that together, we could overpower Mrs. Pl- Drusilla, then I think they would agree,* I said cautiously.

Sounds about right. Hudson smiled at me. Then he bared his teeth playfully. *What are you waiting for?*

Chapter 19. Teamwork

"STOP!" Our two voices sounded brave at first, but the feeling dissolved quickly as the word echoed throughout the yelling people and clang of swords. Only a few people turned toward us, but seeing we were just teens, they turned away.

"I don't think they heard us," I called to Hudson.

"Obviously," he called back, smooth and clear. I caught a flash of gold when he shook his curls and said, "Maybe we shouldn't have Shifted back. We could have sent out a thought to all the dragons that said to stop fighting."

I shook my head. "They still might not listen," I said hopelessly. "But somehow we need to get the message out, before someone gets really hurt." I considered it. Who had a loud voice and trusted me?

"My dad," I said.

"It's hard not to read your thoughts anymore," Hudson told me. "Why do we need your dad?"

I smiled and took a deep breath. "He has a loud voice," I explained. "And he'll trust us. So if we could just find him . . ." My voice faded away as I remembered the swarm of people below me.

"That's an option," Hudson said with a mocking smirk. "But I've got a better one." With deep curiosity I watched as he took two pointer fingers and held them to his mouth. With a sharp exhale, he sent a sound out that pierced the air.

TWEEEET!

The alarmed Houses whipped around to face us. The air filled with unsettling hisses and whispers. I swallowed and glanced at Hudson. At last, I scraped up the courage to speak in front of three angry Houses.

"Hi, I'm Blair Norwillo, Guardian of the Wind Nation." There were some murmurs.

"And I'm Hudson Ignis, member of the Fire Nation," Hudson said calmly. I couldn't help but wonder if really was as relaxed as he seemed, or if inwardly he was freaking out. Like me.

"And we both think you guys have to stop fighting," I said, hoping I sounded like a leader.

"Why?" someone shouted.

"They're the ones who planned the attack!" another person

snapped.

"Quiet!" Hudson yelled. "Look, I know my House. And the Wind Guardian knows heir's," he said, sideways glancing at me. I held back a giggle. Wind Guardian? "We know you all are good people. People with families. People with friends. People with tremendous talent."

"People who shouldn't have to go to war," I finished. I noticed the faces around me, mixes of cold fear but warm hope.

Then someone said it. They were from the Fire Nation, and their voice was deep but nervous. "What about Drusilla?" An anxious shift went through the crowd, especially the fire and Earth Nations.

"Who's Drusilla?" cried someone in a gold uniform.

Suddenly, an arrow whistled through the air. It felt like I was watching things in slow-mo. The arrow was old-fashioned, made of dark, polished wood. The tip was sharp and pointed, and lethal looking silver. It spun so perfectly, twirling, deadly.

And it was going toward Hudson.

I thought I was the only one who saw it. It came from behind us, but then Imogen Ignis jumped forward. A deafening roar filled the air as she Shifted, taking the arrow for Hudson.

"MOM!" Hudson cried. The snowy white dragon whimpered and collapsed to the muddy ground.

"*I* am Drusilla," Mrs. Plia announced, her jolly voice cruel. "And we will be finishing this war."

Chapter 20. Fire Dragons Are Like Cats

Everyone was silent, as if watching a sad movie play before them. Most people cradled worry in their eyes when they looked at Imogen, whimpering as her white scales stained crimson. Hudson sat by her side, angry tears spilling down his face.

"Get out of here, now," Hudson spat. "I never want to see your face again."

Drusilla Plia folded her hands neatly, her teal eyes cold. She smiled tightly. "I'm sorry, Hudson," she said primly. "But I don't take orders from a child. In fact, I don't take orders from anyone except myself."

I glared at Mrs. Plia and decided to Shift. I let out an earth-shaking roar, but Mrs. Plia smiled. "I can do that too," she said pleasantly.

With horror I watched her transform, and a snap sound slapped through the air. Her dragon was humongous, rising twice my size. *How is she so big?* I thought to myself, staring at her blood red body.

Practice, hun, sang a cheery voice. I hated that voice.

Ugh, get out of my head, I growled. I charged at her, but she curled her wing around her body like a shield, and I bounced back harmlessly as if I was a fly.

Unwillingly I Shifted back. "I need BACKUP!" I screamed at the top of my lungs, not caring the fear and shock splayed on everyone else's faces. "If we work together, we can defeat her!"

The first person to run toward me was Ellie. Her face was all bravery and hardness as she sprinted, and soon she Shifted. Her once huge, green, body looked pathetic next to Mrs. Plia's, but maybe together we could . . .

Mrs. Plia took action and her eyes narrowed. Her deep red tail was dotted with thorns, and she swung it around. "DUCK!" Someone screamed, and thankfully only a few spikes lodged into me as I dropped to the ground. But they hurt badly. I roared with pain and immediately knew that the spikes weren't normal ones.

Poison, I heard Ellie think, the thought blanketed with dread. *We should be fine since there weren't many thorns. For now,* she added. *But at least everyone is fighting with us now.*

There are? I looked around me and saw all the dragons had formed a ring around Mrs. Plia, each one a different color.

We're with you, a voice said mentally.

Us too, another said.

I wanted to feel happy as I saw the arrows that flew toward Mrs. Plia, the dragons that spiraled threateningly around her while spewing fire and spinning their tails. But I also watched Mrs. Plia dodge the arrows, spew fire of her own and block the slamming tails with hers.

We need a strategy. I broadcasted my thoughts to everyone except Mrs. Plia. *A plan. She's too ancient to beat in dragon form,* I thought.

So we need to get her back in human form? finished someone.

Exactly, I replied, pleased with my clear leadership.

But she'll just Shift back, protested another voice. *We need her to stay human and then we can trap her.*

You can't just take someone's power away! shouted someone. *If you could . . . well, let's say things would be different right now.* A silence passed over everyone. I could feel people scrolling through the few ideas they had, but none were working.

But she had to have a weakness. All villains did; something they hated, that they were opposed to . . .

Water, I thought suddenly. *She's from the Fire Nation. So she has to have weakness to water. Right?* I asked, aiming the question to the Fire Nation. I was praying that they would say, 'Oh yeah, we have this weakness to water and if we go in it, it takes away all our powers!'

A high-pitched voice twinkled into my head. *We cannot say. We need your alliance first, for this is a secret that could possibly destroy us.*

I bit my lip. *You have the Wind Nation's alliance,* I said cautiously, hoping I was doing the right thing for my House. We twined our tails together, the dragon form of a handshake or a pinky promise. I waited.

You are correct. Finally a Fire Nation's voice echoed throughout my head. It was rushed and nervous. *Long ago,* he started, *our gods warned us to stay away from water. Of course, in human form it was impossible. We had to drink, take showers . . . But as Fire Dragons we got a feeling. One that warned us that water is bad, to stay away from it at all costs.*

I shivered as another dragon took over. *Now, we cannot be sure what it will do. No one has the wit to test it out. But over the years, sometimes our dragons go missing. And we think it's because . . .* She let the statement hang.

Okay, then- Ellie began to say, but was cut off with a roar. A voice slammed into my head, intruding.

Come out and fight like real warriors, Mrs. Plia sneered, then sent out a huge blast of fire. I flew upward just in time to see it set fire to a tree. Mrs. Plia snarled. *Or you can just plan like cowards.* She lunged viciously toward us and everyone flinched.

STAY AWAY! I screamed, spreading out my wings. *Come fight me if you want,* I growled, but I tried to sound like the scared little girl Mrs. Plia wanted me to be. *But stay away from them.*

I spiraled away, the wind whipping against my scales. I didn't dare look behind me, but I prayed that Mrs. Plia was following me. She had to if the plan was going to work. As I flew to the creek nearby, I sent a message to Ellie.

Is Mrs. Plia following me?

It took a second for her to answer. *Yeah. Lead her to the creek, and once she's there we're going to come too.*

Okay, I said.

And once you're at the creek, you have to distract her until we get there. Then we're going to push her into the water from behind and see what happens.

Okay, I repeated.

And then we win the Great War, Ellie sighed. *Hopefully.*

I soon touched down at the creek. It wasn't anywhere near the beauty my creek had, but it would do. The trees were thin above me, so the place felt open. The water was a dark mucky blue-green color and giant, unfriendly rocks loomed under the fast current. I couldn't help but think it was an ominous place.

And then I heard the wing flaps.

Without turning around, I growled low. *Drusilla,* I said, stopping myself before I could call her Mrs. Plia.

Now, hun, that's no way to talk to your future Shifting teacher, Mrs. Plia purred. *I'd prefer being respectful. Don't you agree, Miss. Norwillo?* Her teal eyes gleamed. They looked nothing like Hudson's; instead they were cold and evil.

No! I shrieked, finally whipping myself around. *Where are you?* I asked Ellie. When she didn't answer I continued my stalling. *You're a monster,* I thought. *An ugly, evil monster.*

Thanks for the compliment, Mrs. Plia mocked. *But I learned a long time ago to not take compliments personally.* She lunged, and I rapidly flew away so that I was hovering on top of the water. My heart hammered when she narrowed her eyes; instantly I felt like I was at the bottom of the food chain.

Ellie! I mentally screamed. *NOW!* Twenty dragons seemed to vaporize from treetops, and they slammed with all the force they had into Mrs. Plia. Totally shocked, she fumbled as her wings bent. Clumsily she fell into the creek with a gigantic splash.

I held my breath when everything was silent. Yet suddenly a burning smell protruded from the air.

Is something . . . A voice worried. *Burning?* Then a sizzling sound echoed through the leaves and the bubbling brook. Everyone waited, and then . . . I saw a brown blob of hair. On a head. I swooped and pulled Mrs. Plia out of the water. Everyone gasped as I laid her on the muddy ground.

I- I think she's unconscious, Ellie thought, her mental voice practically silent. *But she's not dead, I don't think.* Her voice shook.

I can hear her heart beating, a female voice announced. *But it's weak. She needs medical attention.* Everyone's thoughts faltered, but someone Shifted back into a person. Freckled face, really short brown hair . . .

Avery stood in front of the crowd of dragons. "She may be evil," Avery said, gesturing to Mrs. Plia. "But we're not." Avery pulled out her phone and dialed 9-1-1. "Help, my stepmother collapsed while we were on a hike . . . yes, yes . . . Okay, come quickly!"

I Shifted back and let a smile creep up my face. "Guys," I said slowly. "I think we won!" The words tasted amazing on my tongue. Once everyone had Shifted back, we cheered. We hugged.

"We did it," I whispered while hugging Ellie.

We had won the Great War.

Chapter 21. Deciphering

Things finally have seemed to calm down.

Well, as calm as things get in my life.

The war was over, and no one had been seriously hurt. Except for Imogen. But she was actually making a great recovery. She had lost a lot of blood, and the wound was deep, but she was in dragon form when it happened, which Ellie told me was really lucky.

"Dragons heal like, three or four times as fast as regular humans," Ellie had explained.

At first Hudson had been down about his mom, but he's all good now. Bummed out that he missed the real fight, though.

"I would love to jump on Drusilla's back," Hudson said mischievously, but he was serious soon afterward. "After what she did to my mom!"

And of course there was the topic of Drusilla Plia.

She wasn't dead, but she wasn't looking too good. She wasn't going to die, they said. In fact, she'd be better in a few weeks.

"And then what?" I had asked Gran. "We just . . . leave her?"

Gran shook her head. "Not at all, Bee-Bee. She'll be jailed for a long time. Not by local authorities, though, because they don't have a clue about us."

I had frowned then. "Then where is she going to be jailed?" I asked confusedly.

Gran's maroon eyes twinkled with a secret. "Well, it's kind of something not many people know about. But it's a specialized jail for the worst criminals. And it's run by these people called the Tribal Police."

"So . . . police just for us?" I said. "That's pretty cool."

But there was one thing that remained unknown; whether or not Mrs. Plia could still Shift. No one knew yet because she hadn't tried it out. Yet I had a feeling that she couldn't when I remembered the sizzling and the smell. It had been like all her power was burning away.

But I had to focus!

I was going over to Hudson's house. It was his birthday in a few weeks, but it felt necessary to celebrate now; after the war and everything. All the Houses would be there, and I was excited.

I had gone casual but not too casual. My hair was pulled back into a claw clip, and I wore jean shorts with a simple white tank top. Plus, some super cute earrings.

As we walked over to Hudson's, I thought about the Prophecy. "It makes sense now," I said to Ellie.

"What does?" She played with her hair, which she'd curled.

"The Prophecy. The Guardian is me, which we already knew. But the 'someone who is not who they seem' and 'betrayal from a leader' is Mrs. Plia. She wasn't a cheery, caring teacher, instead an evil master. She betrayed her students."

"Sure did," Ellie grumbled. "And 'one shall nearly visit the dead' is also Mrs. Plia. The 'bold blood will be shed' must be Imogen, who saved Hudson's life."

"Yeah, that makes sense," I said thoughtfully. "And the 'son of fire' has got to be Hudson, right?"

"Right," Ellie agreed. "Pretty interesting how that all worked out, huh?"

"Yeah," I said as we walked up his sidewalk. The huge house was its pristine white, with the maroon double doors and gold handles.

"Woah," Monnie gaped. "They look like castle doors!"

"Yeah!" Luna chimed in. I smiled.

"Do you want to do the honors?" Dada asked with a smile. "He is your boy, after all." Dada gave me his toothy grin.

"Dada," I groaned. This time, I used the brass knocker. It felt warm in my hands. And I knocked on the door.

Chapter 22. Happy Birthday

"Blair!" Hudson's voice flew throughout the house.

"Hudson!" I yelled back, grinning. His voice sounded amazing; I hadn't heard it since the war.

"Happy Birthday," I said and blushed.

"Thanks," he replied. We walked to the dining room, which was decorated nicely. A banner in big, blocky handwriting said, 'Happy Birthday Hudson'. Balloons bounced slightly on the floor.

"It looks great," I said. "Who decorated?"

Hudson looked at me and grinned. "My mom! She got out of the hospital yesterday," he told me. His voice was smooth like always, but it was impossible not to notice the happiness. His hair shone.

I smiled at his charm. "That's great, Hudson. How is she?"

"Never better," he answered and rolled his eyes. "That's what she's saying, anyway."

I smiled, and suddenly Ellie walked up enthusiastically. "Hey-ya, Hudson!" she announced. "I'm Blair's big sister, Ellie."

Hudson nodded slowly. "You're the one who goes to Birming Dale, right?" he asked coolly.

"That's me," said Ellie, sounding hyper. I felt my face get hot. "It smells great," Ellie continued, her golden eyes shimmering mischievously. "Now, what're we eating tonight? And what flavor is the cake?" she asked.

Hudson laughed, his rosy cheeks brightening. "Pizza for dinner, chocolate cake for dessert," he answered with a smirk.

"Perfect, I'm starving," I admitted sheepishly. I couldn't bear to listen to Ellie talking for one more second, so I wheeled away. I heard Ellie say something before Hudson came after me.

"That's my sister," I said, and I flopped against the table with an exasperated sigh. "In a nutshell."

Hudson smirked. "It's funny to see you get humiliated," he told me. As he teased his azure eyes sparkled. "Your cheeks get all red, you bite your lip. And then you dart away and . . ." He continued on, but I was too busy getting annoyed to listen.

"Oh, shut up," I complained, shoving him. "Can we please go get cake now," I begged.

"You're getting embarrassed again," Hudson pointed out smugly. "See, you're blushing. And your eyes are narrowing . . ." Desperately I tried to stop my heated cheeks, my apparently 'narrowed' eyes.

"I'm getting cake!" I called behind me.

"So am I!"

The dining room was dimly lit when we entered, and everyone was seated. In fact, there were only two seats left. And they were next to each other.

Hudson sat down in front of the cake and I sat next to him. Imogen rushed to light the fourteen candles, and they filled the room with a sweet glow. "Start us off, Hudson!" someone called, and the song began.

Happy Birthday to you, Happy Birthday to you!

I stared at the dimly lit faces around me. Mama, Dada, Gran. Ellie, Monnie, Luna, Atticus. Hudson. Seeing them filled me with a glow; one million times brighter than the candles.

Happy Birthday, dear Hudson . . .

Our voices twined together in a beautiful, happy way. I couldn't help but think that we'd accomplished so much. We brought each other together after hating each other for centuries.

Happy Birthday to you!

And I couldn't help but think that everything was perfect.

ABOUT THE AUTHOR

Theodora (or, Mae-Mae, as her family calls her) lives in Virginia with her parents, three little siblings and her dog. She is eleven years old, but despite her young age, she has a huge love for fantasy writing. Spirit War is her first book to be published publicly, but she has written other stories as well.

Made in the USA
Columbia, SC
10 January 2024

697d2a30-5177-458d-8665-d18c2559ede9R02